Mr.
Peabody's
House

Werewolves, Vampires, and Demons, Oh My

Eve Langlais

New York Times and USA Today Bestselling author

EVELANGLAIS.COM

Copyright and Disclaimer

Published by Eve Langlais
http://www.EveLanglais.com

E-ISBN-13: 978 1988 328 61 4
Print ISBN: 978 1988 328 62 1

ALL RIGHTS RESERVED

Chapter One

"So, when does the debauching begin?" I asked. Kidnapped by gorgeous hunks, my expectations for exceptional seduction and corruption were high.

What a pity my abductors acted so gravely instead of taking off their clothes.

"There will be no debauching."

"Is that your final answer?" To those who wondered if I did it on purpose to drive them crazy...

Duh. Of course, I did. Sometimes, a girl had to make her own fun, especially when people were determined to behave in such a serious, responsible manner. It brought out the absolute best or—depending on your perspective—worst in me.

Looking my most innocent, which my best friend claimed appeared more as if I were about to commit a cardinal sin, I asked, "Is it true you're werewolves?"

None of my kidnappers deigned to reply.

"Do you howl at the moon?"

A question ignored.

As if I'd let that deter me from trying to make conversation. "Bark at cats?"

Again, no response.

Undaunted, I kept peppering my abductors, anything to make them talk—or snap. "Chase cars? Pee to mark your territory? Ever get sprayed by a skunk? Is it true you need to soak in tomato juice to get the stench out?"

A practical question they also chose to ignore.

"Are you leg humpers? Do you like it doggy style?"

One of my abductors developed a slight twitch.

I tossed out the big guns. "Have you been neutered? Do you still have your balls?"

Finally, I got a reaction. The big dude, and I mean *big* in every sense of the word, turned to look at me.

Someone hand me a fan. Tanned, with brown hair and eyes, Mr. In-Charge was a caramel fantasy I wanted to lick from head to toe. Especially the spots in between.

"Would you stop that?"

With a grin that promised I wouldn't, I purred, "Stop what? Just making conversation. About time you remembered I was here."

"How could I forget? You never shut up."

"You're the one who kidnapped me. Deal with it."

"We didn't kidnap you," he growled, the low rumble perhaps a result of his animalistic pedigree.

"Did you or did you not sandwich me between your big, burly bodies and whisk me off

4

to your lair?" And by lair, I meant house on the rim of town, not a cool cave or aerie.

"We were tasked with protecting you."

Did he have to sound so annoyed by it? He might not be enamored with the job he'd been assigned, but I said *too bad*. I was having the time of my life even if I still wore all my clothes.

To those who huffed, "Hussy," they could suck it. What else was a girl with blood running through her veins to think or fantasize about when guarded by three ungodly handsome hunks? Yes, I said three. Tall, broad dudes with serious muscles and chiseled faces.

My va-jay-jay was swooning—or possibly drowning. Whatever the case, my panties were soaked and not from pee, even if some girls might have wet themselves if confronted by three guys who were a little bit on the hairy side. Hairy as in they were werewolves.

Real ones, not the kind that wore a fur suit and faked howling on Halloween.

Werewolves really existed.

Turned out humans weren't alone on this planet, and did the shit ever hit the fan when we found out.

As to how it happened, a little while back, shapeshifters and other weird creatures came out of the fairy tale closet to tell the world they existed. They didn't really have a choice when the little orphan girl the forest rangers had rescued from the woods turned into a wolf pup on live television. Apparently, the bright lights set her off.

Out of fear the government would dissect

her to death, the leader of the wolves, some older, hot dude who called himself an Alpha, stepped forward.

People kind of lost their minds.

Cute, itty-bitty wolfgirl wasn't so scary. Big-ass wolfman? Humanity's deepest fears and superstitions bubbled to the surface.

For a while, panic drove humans a little crazy. Sales of guns and silver went through the roof. But, eventually, the chaos settled down as folks realized werewolves were just like us, only hairier.

The memes that flooded the Internet as a result were epic—gallon-sized bottles of Nair for the werewolf in your life, clogged drain jokes, you name it, the Internet had a pic for it.

The jokes about them fetching balls and chasing cars died down only when the newest scandal rocked the media. The Internet just about broke the day the world discovered mermaids were real—and really not as hot as the sailors used to claim. Made you wonder just how much grog they used to drink before they tried to bang one. It definitely explained why so many men claimed va-jay-jays smelled like fish.

Knowing Lycans—the fancy word werewolves used to classify themselves—existed was one thing. Actually meeting one in the flesh and multiplied by three?

I could have howled in excitement. It made me wish I'd worn something more provocative like my red sweater or at least my T-shirt that said *Huff and Puff* with an arrow pointing down.

While my abductors looked human, I had to wonder, did they feel human on the outside?

"Would you stop stroking me?" the leader of the crew barked. Human bark, not wolf.

"You're not as furry as expected." Despite the canine gene, the Lycan dude's forearms were actually pretty smooth and hair-free.

Did that lack of fur extend to all their body parts? My gaze might have strayed south of his belt buckle.

"He's not hairy at all, but I am," McHunky number two stated with a wink.

The guys actually had names. The leader was Dale—he of the tanned skin, brown hair, and brown eyes. Mike was the serious beast with the dark locks and killer blue eyes that kept glaring at me. Then there was Sebastian or, as I'd secretly named him, McHunky, with his long hair held back in a ponytail and the most amazing green eyes.

Dale, Mike, and Sebastian. Sounded like strippers to me. Looked like strippers, too, in their skintight T-shirts and hip-hugging jeans. Made me wonder how they'd react if presented with a pole.

Would they dance around it in tiny G-strings, or treat it like a fire hydrant and pee on it?

I kind of wanted to find out, but a glance around didn't show any kind of pole in their place. Nor any full-length mirrors or glittering disco balls.

"This is fucking unbelievable," growled Mike.

He was the grumpy one of the three, sporting a scowl from the moment we met. It totally made me want to turn his frown upside down, but when I grabbed his ass and goosed him, he didn't even squeak.

"If you don't like having me around, then maybe you shouldn't have kidnapped me, Mr. Grumpy Pants."

"We didn't kidnap you," sighed Dale.

"I know," said with a roll of my eyes. "You are *protecting* me from evil."

At least, that was what Chloe, my BFF, claimed when we returned after an epic day of shopping to find her place trashed.

Someone, or something—cue the ominous music—had totally demolished her place, and there was concern that whoever or whatever did it would come after Chloe again. If they couldn't find her, then what better way to hurt Chloe than coming after me, her bestest friend in the whole wide world?

Seriously, we'd been best buds since kindergarten. She was the Chewie to my Han Solo. The wingwoman in my quest for dick.

Except, as it turned out, she was better at the holy quest for cock, seeing as how Chloe snared two guys—a vampire, and a werewolf—totally one-upping me.

Bitch. Yes, I was jealous. Totally green-eyed with it. But I could still redeem myself and beat her at this game. After all, I was in the custody of three werewolves and totally down for some hot and sweaty action.

Only one problem with my plan. The three dudes assigned to me pretended disinterest.

Totally not cool. Utterly unheard of.

In today's modern world, where men outnumbered women five to one—the theory for that disparity being we'd not had any great big wars in a while—meant women had their pick of dudes. Hell, there were even laws encouraging women to marry in multiples. The tax breaks were amazing.

No woman, from legal-aged to ancient, lacked for male companionship if desired. I couldn't go anywhere without men hitting on me.

Alas, for all my experience—much of it exaggerated so my best friend wouldn't know I scared most guys off with my shining disposition—I'd yet to find even one guy that I liked who could stand me for more than one night.

Sure, they had sex with me, but…you know how guys say they will call?

Mine never do.

Sad. Actually, kind of ego crushing, but I wasn't the type of person to let that get me down.

If the men I met didn't realize how awesome I was, if they couldn't handle a woman with spirit, then screw 'em. *I don't need them.*

If only I believed that lie, then maybe I'd stop torturing myself.

"Fear not, baby, we'll keep you safe." Sebastian winked. He was the flirtiest of the three, his sexy green eyes enough to melt the panties off any woman with a heartbeat.

"How long do we have to babysit her?" asked Mike.

The fact that Mike termed a bodyguard job "babysitting" brought out the imp in me.

I grabbed my hair on each side of my head,

fisting it into pigtails, and jutted my lower lip. "I'm bored. Wanna play with me?" I batted my lashes, and he turned away.

Dale did his best to not smile.

My antics proved hard for him to resist. I was that cute.

Annoying, but adorable.

"We'll watch her for as long as I say," Dale announced. "Which is until it's deemed safe for her to leave."

Mr. Grumpy just wouldn't give in gracefully. "Just because you owe Pete a favor isn't a reason to rope us in."

Pete, for the uninformed, was Chloe's werewolf boyfriend. They'd met over an indecent exposure case. He peed on a neighbor's flowers, and she defended him.

So romantic.

Flopping onto a couch that had seen better days, I sighed. "If you don't want to watch me, then maybe I should just leave."

I didn't mean it. Why would I want to leave the most exciting thing to ever happen to me?

"You're not going anywhere."

Not even nirvana? How disappointing.

Twirling a lock of my hair around a finger, I did what I did best. Asked questions. "So, who or what exactly do you think went psycho on Chloe's place? Ogre?" Not as cute as the *Shrek* version according to the documentary I watched. "Dwarf?" Small but stocky with mighty tempers, especially when drunk. "Rabid rabbit?" Hold on, wasn't that a video game?

"It was a demon," Dale announced.

To which Mike scoffed, "Those don't exist."

"On the contrary"—Dale shook his head—"they do. We just haven't seen or heard of any for centuries."

"Maybe we haven't seen any because they don't exist." What a surprise, Mike argued.

"I've got it on good authority that they do," Dale argued back.

"Fine, let's say they do exist. I thought they liked eating witches, so why would a demon be going after a human?" The disparagement in Mike's tone couldn't have been clearer.

As I jumped in to defend my BFF with a, "Hey, humans taste delicious." I frowned at Mike. "Why shouldn't a demon go after Chloe? She is, after all, the second most awesome person in the world."

"Let me guess, you're first?" Mike drawled with an arched brow.

So sexy, but my lust for him wouldn't let the insult slide. "I'm third on that list, actually. My meemaw is number one."

Grandma had raised me to be the perfect person I was today. Now, if only people would value it. Other than my meemaw, only Chloe and her parents appreciated my unique blend of outspoken sarcasm and blunt charm. Even my daddy couldn't handle me.

It would make me sadder except Meemaw said, "He's a pussy, forget about him." So I did…most of the time.

"Your meemaw should have taught you manners," grumbled Mike. "Who the hell goes around asking people if they bark at the moon?"

"I said howl, and I don't see the problem. I mean, if you asked me if I read books, I wouldn't take offense, even if I say the only good book is a movie adaptation."

"You are completely insane." Mike shook his head at me.

"No, she's not," Sebastian jumped in. "I think she's interesting"—that earned him a smile—"for a human."

The smile disappeared faster than my morals after a few glasses of wine. "Are you guys always so speciest?" Yeah, I made the word up. What else to call these men who seemed to think they could look down on me and not just because they were taller?

Being tall didn't mean I couldn't take them out at the knees.

So I did. I dove from the couch and hit Sebastian around the thighs, toppling him—timber!

He hit the ground, and before he could recover, I scrambled up his body until I straddled him.

"You're an ass," I stated with my arms crossed under my boobs.

He didn't reply.

Not one word.

And a slow smile pulled at my lips because, despite my humanity, he really did think I was cute. The proof pressed against my va-jay-jay, evident even through my pants and his jeans.

Alas, I couldn't be a normal girl and bat my lashes or say something adorable and sexy.

I was just me. Brenda Jane Whittaker, and I ruined the moment with, "Holy shit, are you hiding a tail in your pants?"

Dale Interlude

Why me?

When Pete had called and said he needed a favor, Dale said yes. What else to say to the lone wolf who could have been Alpha if he chose?

Dale owed the other man—who, in many ways, was like a brother to him—too much to say no. So he'd grabbed his best buds and hurried over to an apartment building in midtown, where he met the most vexing, adorable, annoyingly tempting vixen ever.

How could someone who didn't even reach his chin with bouncy blonde hair, vivid emerald eyes, and the cutest bow-shaped lips be so raunchy and outspoken?

Every time Brenda opened her mouth, she said something utterly outrageous.

And yet, she didn't do it maliciously. Humor glinted in her gaze, her lips curved in a constant smile. Even Mike's acerbic nature didn't bring her down.

Although, little Miss Bite-Sized did manage to bring Sebastian down.

The poor guy lay under her, frozen in place by indecision and a good dose of lust.

Dale could understand that. Since the moment he'd met Brenda, he'd found himself shaken by all kinds of feelings and urges.

Urges that didn't involve protecting her pert little ass or guarding her banging body. No, things like grabbing that perfect butt, and caressing the sweet flesh filled his mind.

I shouldn't think of her like that. Shouldn't, and yet he couldn't help himself. It didn't help that she flirted constantly in between her outrageous questions.

And now, she'd committed the cardinal sin. Asked a werewolf in man shape if he had a tail.

"Well?" she asked, cocking her head. She wiggled. "Is it big? Long? Thick?" She batted her lashes, her lips curved with wickedness.

His voice husky and low, Sebastian said, "Perhaps I should show you."

Before Sebastian could indeed whip it out—and get a fist to his face because, for some reason, the idea of his friend touching this woman made Dale see red—Dale intervened, picking Brenda up and depositing her on the couch.

"Behave," he admonished.

"Where's the fun in that?"

Where indeed?

To avoid further distraction, Dale signaled to his friends. They headed across the room, as far as they could get from Brenda to regroup and recover.

But her scent followed. It permeated every part of the space. Made him feel things. Things he shouldn't feel for someone he was tasked with protecting.

"That woman is a lunatic. I swear if I have to stay around her much longer, she's going to drive me bat-shit crazy," Mike admitted in a frustrated low voice.

"Yeah, she is crazy, but damn, what a body," sighed Sebastian with a longing look in Brenda's direction. "I swear, she makes me want to…"

He didn't finish the sentence. He didn't need to because Dale understood how he felt.

He felt the same lust.

For one woman.

Sharing was supposed to be caring, but not when it came to chicks.

Despite his close friendship with his brothers from another mother, Dale didn't subscribe to the new world order where women indulged in reverse harems.

In his world, a relationship involved one man, one woman.

And if Dale couldn't have her, neither could Sebastian. "Paws off the woman. You know we can't do anything."

"But you heard her. She's definitely interested."

"Give your head a shake. We can't do her," Mike snapped. "Mission. Remember?"

"Temporary mission," Sebastian corrected with a glance over at the girl.

He had a point. Once the demon was caught, she wouldn't be their responsibility any longer.

She'd be free to do as she chose, and so would they.

They could choose to chase her. Pin her.

Lick her from head to foot.

Claim her and make her mine.

But only if he got to her first. Good thing he was fast on four feet.

May the best wolf win.

Chapter Two

How is a girl supposed to win over a werewolf when he won't even come close?

My initial euphoria over getting Sebastian to blush, and show with his body what he truly thought of me, didn't last.

As usual, my big mouth just had to get involved, and not in a way that saw me on my knees making him grab my hair and moan, "Oh my God."

Not to brag, but I really knew how to pleasure a cock. I blamed all the Popsicles I'd sucked over the course of my life.

Not that I'd ever get a chance to show any of these guys my suction skills. I had managed in my usual elegant way to frighten off all the eligible men in the area.

Look at the big bad wolves, clustered at the far end of the room, as if I had cooties. Didn't they wear collars for that?

Since they seemed more interested in each other than me, I studied the place I found myself in.

The house was a definite bachelor pad—a solid, two-story brick residence on a quiet suburban street, only two blocks over from a dog park. Coincidence?

The entire place had a *guy* vibe to it. From the scratched parquet floors to the furniture that didn't match, it lacked a woman's touch.

Did this mean they were single? A lusty mind and body wanted to know.

The walls were a dull beige, covered at random with framed prints of metal bands and sexpots: Guns 'N' Roses, Nine Inch Nails, and one of Harley Quinn and her bat.

I'd dressed as her for Halloween. Got six marriage proposals that night. Three were for green card status, though, so they didn't really count.

An epic, man-sized television took up a huge chunk of wall and was longer than I was. No surprise, sitting under it were two game consoles. Xbox and PlayStation. I preferred a rousing game of *Clash of Clans* or *Candy Crush* myself.

The coffee table, a battered wooden thing with one short leg propped on an unopened can of peas, had the surface covered in remotes, game cases, and a box of Hot Rods—the spicy pepperoni stick variety.

The couch I sat on was some plaid monstrosity, huge, long, and surprisingly comfortable if shabby. It reminded me of the one in the fraternity I used to party at while in college, except this couch smelled of men's cologne, not beer, weed, and sex.

Speaking of sex, despite Sebastian's erection, I really began to wonder if these three close friends were more than friends. I mean, hello, they lived together. Did they play hide the sausage when no humans were around?

I didn't have a problem with gay men. I just wished they'd tell me upfront so I wouldn't waste my time trying to get in their pants.

A phone rang, not mine, and Dale answered, too quiet for me to hear. Whatever was said caused a stir. Off they moved, all three of them sliding into the kitchen, my glimpse of the place brief as the door to the space swung shut after them.

Left alone to my own devices—never a good idea—I decided, fuck this shit.

Just because Chloe's boyfriends thought her demon stalker might come after me wasn't reason enough for me to stick around with three guys who obviously didn't give a damn if I lived or died.

And really, what were the chances a demon would come after me?

Then again, if one did, at least I'd get more action than I was right now.

Feeling ignored, and bored, which was usually my excuse whenever I got pulled in front of the principal and now my boss at work, I left.

Walked right out that front door and marched down the steps and paused on the sidewalk, looking left and right.

This late at night, not a single thing stirred. Nobody walked the sidewalks. The houses on the street were almost all dark. Only one had the blue, flashing glow of a television on behind closed curtains.

Flagging a cab seemed unlikely, so I pulled

out my phone and swiped my screen to find my Uber app.

Before my ride could arrive, my departure was noticed.

"Get back inside," Dale ordered me.

So funny. I didn't do orders. Unless they were of the sexual variety. For some odd reason, I tended to have a submissive side when it came to sex.

I checked my email.

Someone didn't like being ignored. Welcome to the club.

"Brenda, I said get your ass back inside."

"No, thank you." See, I did have some manners.

Dale didn't care. "Get back inside, right now."

He sounded like the father that didn't stick around.

I ignored him like I disregarded my own dad the rare times he came by to see me after he'd ditched my mother. A budding scientist who was going places, he didn't have the time or inclination to deal with the woman he'd gotten pregnant. Deadbeat jerk. Knocked her up and then skipped town for college. Mother had me alone and died two weeks later in a fluke accident while taking me to the doctor's for a check-up.

Meemaw got custody, and my dad didn't even fight her for it. I owed everything to that crotchety old lady, and I knew what she'd tell me to do in this situation.

Tell him to fuck off.

But I was a lady—for the moment. So, instead, I gave him the silent treatment.

There wasn't any sound, and yet I knew Dale had come off the steps and stalked toward me using his super werewolf sneaking powers.

I whirled and glared at him. "Stop right there." Pulling my hand free from my purse, I aimed my can of pepper spray at him. A single girl never left home without it.

He stopped and cocked his head. "You wouldn't."

"You don't want to dare me." I could never resist a challenge. It got me in so much trouble in college.

"Put the can down."

"What if I don't want to?"

"Let's go inside to talk about it."

He should have said the magic words, "*Let's go inside and get naked.*"

"No."

"What's the problem?"

"The problem is that you and your boyfriends have made it obvious you'd rather do anything but watch over me." Or do me. "So I'm going to fix the situation and leave."

"We promised to protect you."

I shrugged. "Yeah, but I didn't promise to let you do it. And I'm not in the mood to stick around where I'm not wanted. I'm sure you and your bros will be happy the *human* is going home." I might have sneered the word.

"Are you really peeved about Sebastian's remark?" His brows rose in surprise. "You're the one who wouldn't stop with the dog jokes."

"I was asking about your habits because I think it's cool. You're the ones acting like I'm diseased or something. Treating me like I'm some desperate, pathetic human who can't get laid." Okay, the last part was on me, not them. Still, though, this evening could have been a lot more fun if they'd just all stripped and made me their Venus for the night.

"We're supposed to protect you, not seduce you. Pete would have our heads if we disrespected you in any way."

I blinked. "How is worshipping my body disrespectful?"

A grin tugged at his lips. "Because doing dirty things would mean we're shirking our responsibility."

"Does this mean we could do dirty things if you didn't have to protect me?"

"Possibly."

"Even if I'm human?"

He shrugged. "Not your fault you're not a bitch."

At that, I couldn't help but snicker. "Dude, that is seriously fucked up."

"I would say that's par for this evening. Now, would you please come back inside?"

"No." I whirled around and began to walk. No idea where I'd go. Didn't care either.

Dale didn't let me get far. Sweeping in behind me, he simply grabbed me and upended me over his shoulder.

For a moment, I was too shocked to act.

Pleasure at his manhandling swept through me. About time he did something hot and exciting.

Except he'd made it clear we weren't going to have fun, so this was just him being bossy.

I didn't do bossy.

I clenched my hands together and slammed him in the lower back.

"Let me go."

He grunted but kept walking.

I thrashed, undulating my body, kicking my legs, slamming my fists, yet he didn't drop me. His arm remained firmly anchored over my thighs.

"Put me down, Scooby-Doo. Right this instant," I demanded. His barbaric manhandling was as arousing as it was frustrating because I knew he didn't carry me back inside for debauchery.

Since flailing didn't work, I took a bite, a hard bite of flesh covered by a T-shirt.

"Harder, baby. I don't think you left a mark."

Not exactly the reaction I'd hoped for. So I resorted to more vile methods. I licked my finger and then contorted my arm, trying to wet willy his ear.

Ducking his head, he exclaimed, "Don't you dare."

I dared. My wet digit found its mark and wiggled.

Smack.

The firm spank on my bottom froze me.

He spanked me?

"Does this mean you've changed your mind about sex?" I asked, suddenly hopeful.

"Behave, or I'll do it again."

Did he think I was a child he could discipline?

"Unhand me this instant," I screeched. My annoyance levels had skyrocketed.

It should be noted I wasn't against spanking, in the right situation—that being naked and used as foreplay.

But as a tactic to subdue me?

Oh, hell no.

"Don't make me smack you again."

"Go ahead, and just for the record, you can forget doing any dirty things with me now, Scooby. I don't like you at all."

"Funny, it doesn't smell that way."

The fact that he could smell my arousal shut me up.

Only once he made it back inside the house did he finally set me down.

Then he thought he could order me around some more. He gave me a stern look and said, "You are not to—"

"Excuse me, do you really think I give a damn what you have to say?" I didn't allow time for a retort. I threw myself at him.

Small but mighty, that was what my coach called me. A touch over five feet meant I lived in almost perpetual height disadvantage. So my private self-defense tutor, paid for by Meemaw when I came home crying one day about the boys teasing me at school—back when I wore glasses and braces and sported a terrible case of acne— taught me how to fight dirty.

Also known as winning against bigger, more muscled odds.

What my instructor didn't teach me was how to take down a werewolf.

The fucking guy just stood there taking my hits. Since he was tall, my jabs to his face barely rocked him. His rock-hard stomach didn't dent at my punches—and my fist throbbed after a particularly solid hit.

So I whacked him in the solar plexus. That got him to gasp, and my knee went straight for his jewels.

"Fucking hell!" he bellowed.

I smiled with triumph instead of escaping and thus found my arms seized behind my back in a firm grip.

"What the hell is wrong with you?" Mike snarled.

Lots of things, apparently. I rammed my head back but didn't do much damage against his chest. But my foot had no problem slamming his instep, drawing a sharp cry from Mike.

"That's enough, kitten," Dale yelled.

Kitten? Was he trying to soften me up with a cute nickname? "I am not your pussy." I stared at Dale defiantly.

"Are you sure? Because you certainly spit and yowl like one," Mike interjected.

"Let me go so I can scratch your eyes out," I hissed.

"Can't we all just get along?" Sebastian asked.

"No!" We might have hollered it in tandem.

"Let her go," Dale ordered with a wave of his hand.

"She's a menace to society."

"I'm pretty sure we can handle her."

Ha, that's what he thought.

Mike loosened his grip, and I thanked him by ramming my elbow in his gut.

While Mike cursed under his breath, I announced, "I'm leaving." I went to move past Dale, but he sidestepped me.

"You can't go yet. It's not safe."

"It's not safe here either."

"We haven't harmed you. You, on the other hand, seem to be doing your best to hurt us."

What could I say? I'd lost my delicate fucking flower gene somewhere along the way. "Maybe if you weren't trying to keep me here against my will, I wouldn't have to resort to protecting myself."

"What are we supposed to do when you won't listen to reason?"

I tilted my chin. "I want to go home. And as a grown woman, that is my choice. So unless you're going to sit on me all night, you can't stop me."

"Actually, I can stop you. Mike. Get the rope."

Rope?

What?

Once again, my mouth got me in trouble.

In short order, despite all my best fighting moves—and I pulled out some doozies that left bruises, a fat lip, and a possible black eye by the morning—I was tethered, both arms stretched to the side and overhead, to the headboard of a bed.

Fully clothed.

And then left alone.

Could this evening get any worse?

Sebastian Interlude

The screaming invectives, a non-stop litany of things Brenda would shove into holes that never saw the sun, erupted in a steady stream. Some of them quite imaginative, and painful.

Sebastian couldn't help but stare at the ceiling, a twinge of guilt making him wonder if they'd done the right thing. "Do you really think we needed to tie her up?" As far as he was concerned, the only time restraints should be used was in the presence of massage oil, dim lighting, and feathers.

"We didn't have a choice. The brat is awfully feisty." The almost admiring words came from Mike, which caused Dale to arch a brow.

"A compliment at last?"

The scowl quickly returned. "Just saying she's no pushover. Doesn't mean shit."

"Holy shit, you think she's hot," Sebastian prodded.

"If you like bite-sized morsels."

"I do believe that's a yes." Which kind of fucked with Sebastian's plans to ask the girl out. He'd taken a shine to her, but if Mike had, too…that could cause friction.

"What Mike thinks doesn't matter. We're

still on protective detail," Dale reminded.

Protective and investigative. Before the call arrived for Dale and his crew to protect one delectable ass, they'd been assigned to help investigate a series of murders.

A bunch of dead witches usually wouldn't bother the Lycan community, except the thing doing the killing wasn't being subtle about it. There were certain rules the non-humans had to follow, and one of them was: don't leave a mess.

But if a demon were doing it, then it probably hadn't gotten that memo. Speaking of which, was it just Sebastian, or was there something inherently wrong about demons walking the earth?

"Can we stop focusing on the girl and try to get back to business? Did we ever get a report back on who blew up the warehouse?" Mike asked.

In the course of their secret investigation into the witch murders, a tip had come in, telling them to check out a certain derelict building down in the factory district.

Dale shook his head. "Nothing was found. The forensics the cops ran came up empty. The wizards who combed the spot didn't find shit either."

"I doubt a demon set an explosive charge," Mike remarked. "If"—and his tone made it sound doubtful— "a demon is involved, he'd probably use magic."

"If we assume the demon or whoever is killing those witches didn't set it, then who did?" Sebastian asked.

Dale shrugged. "No idea. Nor can we ascertain a motive."

"If there is an actual demon walking around, then the person that summoned it is probably the one fucking with us. But why?"

"Why else other than to ensure they can conquer the world?" Sebastian uttered an evil "muahahahaha" that his friends didn't find funny at all.

He'd wager Brenda would have, though. She had a great sense of humor.

And a banging body.

"What I still don't get is, why call a demon? I mean it's not like you can exactly order them around. Or keep them as a pet."

"Are you suddenly a demon expert?" Mike asked sarcastically.

"No, but I did do some research. By all indications, they are vicious killing machines with a thirst for blood."

"Witch blood," Mike corrected.

"And flesh." Sebastian shuddered, recalling the crime scene photos of the murders. Even when he went full wolf and hunted, he drew the line at eating his kills raw. It was why he kept a camping stove and a box full of spices in the trunk of his car.

"Again, hypothetically speaking, if we are dealing with a demon, how do you kill it?" Mike asked.

Dale rolled his shoulders. "No idea. I imagine if it's flesh and blood then decapitation will probably work."

"Or will it just grow a new head?" Sebastian played devil's advocate.

"I'm sure the wizards will know," was Dale's reply.

Knowing Pete, he'd probably already contacted them as soon as they found out about the creature.

"They might know, but it doesn't mean they'll tell anyone," Mike said with a snort.

Wizards were the more learned version of witches. In other words, they went to a university for magic, whereas witches learned their craft in the kitchen using a plain old pot on a stove instead of a fancy cauldron. Only rarely did humans ever get invited to learn at their prestigious schools, mostly because pure-bred humans had no magic.

What did this mean? If a human had magic, then chances were someone in their family had banged an elf or someone else strong in power like a dryad or a djinn.

Also, contrary to popular belief, magic didn't work with a simple wave of the hand like the stories claimed. A true witch's or wizard's power came from potions and incantations. Ritualistic mumbo jumbo that influenced forces they couldn't see.

In other words, weird shit that people really shouldn't meddle with.

The upstairs had grown silent, Brenda having given up cursing and pleading for them to let her go. Or had she managed to escape?

Sebastian wouldn't put it past her. For a petite thing, she possessed a lot of gumption. Still, though, tying her up did seem rather harsh, but Dale did have a point. Short of sitting on her, how could they prevent her from leaving?

Locking her in a room wouldn't work. The windows would provide escape to someone determined.

Sitting and staring at her would have driven them all bat-shit crazy. Mike might have tried to kill her if she started asking him more dog questions.

So, they'd tied her up.

Left her helpless, and alone. What if something came through the window?

Sebastian stood. "Maybe we should check on Brenda."

"Good idea. I'll go." Dale strode to the stairs and took them two at a time. He didn't come back down.

Sebastian's plan to appear as the good guy having backfired, he paced the living room.

"Do you think we'll get a chance to fight the demon or whatever it is hunting the witches?" he asked Mike.

"Are you that anxious to scar up that pretty face?"

"Look who's calling who pretty. I saw the phone number that female cop shoved at you when you were checking shit out at that crime scene."

Mike made a face. "Bloody humans looking to slum." Mike really had little patience with non-Lycans.

Perhaps Sebastian wouldn't have to worry

about him chasing Brenda after all.

"What do you think Dale's doing up there?" he asked, staring at the ceiling.

"Maybe he's getting his balls handed to him." Mike growled the words and clenched his fists.

"Maybe I should go help him."

"Why not admit you just want to spy on the blonde?"

"Why spy when I can openly look? Unlike you and Dale, I'm not afraid to say I think she's hot."

"Until she opens her mouth."

"She's forthright."

"Rude."

"Gee, kind of reminds me of someone I know." Sebastian's pointed look at Mike only made him scowl.

"You're an asshole."

"I'm going to check on Dale."

Taking the steps a pair at a time, Sebastian hit the second floor and stopped. Dale sat in front of the door to his bedroom, the room they'd stashed Brenda in.

"What's up, boss? Is the girl all right?"

"She's fine."

"Then why do you look like someone gave you shitty news?"

Dale shrugged. "Guess I'm feeling a little guilty."

"A little?" Sebastian slid down the wall to sit across from him.

"Maybe tying her to the bed was a bit

harsh."

"She did try to leave, as well as attempt to emasculate you and Mike."

Dale shrugged. "Can you blame her?"

Not really. "What are we going to do about her?"

"Noth—" Dale stopped mid-word and pulled out his phone, which vibrated with fierce urgency.

Signaling to Sebastian, they headed away from the door before answering.

It was Pete with news about the demon.

And a warning.

Chapter Three

When my captors entered, I woke instantly. Sue me for napping. I was tired and obviously not going anywhere—or getting any action.

As they clomped into the room, I glared at Dale, the man responsible for me being tied up like a heifer. "Come to torture me some more?"

"Only if you deserve it."

I gaped because the prick didn't even deny it. "Jerk. What happened to you promising Pete you'd protect me?"

"We did. And you'll be glad to know Pete just called to say we're clear."

"What?"

"What he means to say," Sebastian interjected, "is the demon was killed."

Dale picked up the story. "Pete and Anthony managed to keep the creature busy, and a collective of senior wizards destroyed it."

The wizard thing really begged for more questions, but I had a more pressing query. "So, Chloe is safe?" Which then led my brain to the realization that, "I can go home?"

"Yes, you can leave." Dale inclined his head, and his two henchmen circled to either side of the bed to release me.

As soon as I was free, I bounced to my feet, shouting, "Freedom!"

And then I launched myself at Dale.

He caught me instead of dropping me or hitting the floor, which, I will admit, was super hot. I wrapped my legs around him, but instead of plastering him with kisses, I hit him.

A lot. While haranguing him.

He deserved it.

Tying me up.

Leaving me alone.

He didn't defend himself, just sighed as Mike and Sebastian peeled me off him.

"Asshole. I hope you get a rash and have to wear a cone for a month. No, make that a year," I yelled as they dragged me out of the room.

"I don't get rashes," he replied, his calm demeanor annoying me further.

"I hope you get bitten by a rabid squirrel."

"You already tried, kitten. You couldn't even break skin."

Oooh, insult me, would he?

"Let me at him." I pulled, but the guys held me firmly.

"What should we do with her?" Mike asked.

Well, given their actions, they wouldn't be doing me.

I stopped struggling. "I am going home now."

"I'll drive you."

The offer came from Sebastian, the same guy who'd helped tie me up.

The size of his erection for me couldn't

erase that fact.

"No, thank you. I'll take a cab home."

"I'll drive." Dale grabbed his keys. He didn't hold on to them for long, seeing as how I kicked them out of his hand.

"I don't want to be anywhere near you guys." I might be desperate for love, but I had some self-respect. And pride wouldn't let me accept anything from these dogs. "If you'll give me my purse, I can handle things from here."

"But—"

A sharp look from Dale and Sebastian bit back what Mike planned to say.

My arms were released, and my purse handed to me, along with my shoes.

I didn't look any of them in the eyes as I prepared to leave. I didn't need them trying to con me with their puppy faces.

Obviously, any fantasy I'd had about getting with one or all of them wasn't happening. Best to leave now while I had a shred of dignity.

Leaving with class didn't stop my parting shot. "Don't forget, summer is coming. Better visit your vet for your heartworm pills."

And with that, I slammed the door shut.

Dale didn't come running out to drag me back in.

Mike didn't insist I apologize or accuse me of rudeness.

Even Sebastian didn't come loping after me with his tongue lolling.

I knew how to deal with my old friend disappointment. I fed it the chocolate bar stashed in my purse.

The ride home didn't take long, a regular cab showing up before I could even whip out my phone to call for one. A taxi dropped off some staggering folks at a house across the way, and I hopped in before it could take off.

The driver was more than happy to help me, his kind smile easing my bruised ego. A pity he was at least sixty years old and, according to his ring finger, married.

As soon as I got to my place, I tackled my persistent disappointment with food. I ate a pair of waffles—blueberry leggo-my-Eggo kind. Showered. Ate two more waffles, plain but smothered in Cheez Whiz. All the while, I tried to see how I'd gone wrong.

Wrong times three. How had I gone from starting last night in the presence of three eligible men—or so I assumed, I'd never confirmed their relationship status or sexuality—to alone, and unmolested.

Not that any of it mattered. Guys who thought they could just manhandle me—fully clothed and without offering a happy ending—didn't merit a second chance.

A girl had to have some standards. Now, if only my prideful stance didn't leave me feeling a little down.

I needed to talk to someone who'd totally be on my side. I needed my BFF.

When Chloe answered, though, I first asked her, "Holy fuck, what happened last night? I hear the demon got cremated."

"Oh my gawd, Brenda," Chloe squealed. "It was the scariest fucking thing."

I twirled a length of blonde hair as Chloe told me about her most excellent demon adventure.

It turned out Pete's neighbor's cat was the demon, and it came after Chloe, intent on making her its victim.

"It came right after me, Brenda. And it had huge fangs."

It sounded terrifying. Panty wetting in a urine kind of way, and yet…when Chloe recounted how her lovers came to her rescue and literally tore pieces out of the demon determined to eat her, I couldn't help but sigh.

"You're so lucky."

"Lucky to be alive," she grumbled.

"Lucky because you found two guys who love you enough to face a minion of Hell."

"Anthony says Hell doesn't exist." Anthony being her vampire lover who worked as a district attorney.

Did I mention he was fucking hot? My best friend had hit the boyfriend jackpot.

"Hell might not exist, but apparently, demons do so I'm going to call bullshit on his answer," I argued because I wasn't about to agree with anything a man said today. Changing the subject, I asked, "How are you doing?" Because, despite the happy ending to her adventure, I could hear a hint of hysteria in her voice.

"Oh, you know, feeling a little off-kilter, what with a demon wanting to kill me and then my boyfriends turning into monsters and eating the demon instead."

"Monsters?"

Chloe sighed. "Wrong choice of words. They're not monsters. But it was scary seeing what they could do, Brenda. I mean, you hear about werewolves, but seeing one go all primitive, and then Anthony getting all fanged up…"

"Kind of freaked you out?" I prodded. "Made you feel all too human?"

I could kind of relate.

"I know it's crazy. I mean, I love them, and they love me. Who cares if they have special powers?"

Judging by the tone of her voice, it bothered her. "Are you scared of them?"

It took Chloe a moment before she replied. "No. I'm not." Then more strongly. "They would never hurt me."

"If they wouldn't hurt you, then why are you being stupid?" I didn't hesitate to tell her. I'd never seen Chloe more alive and happy than with these two guys. The fact that they were different than she was shouldn't make a difference.

"I am being stupid, aren't I?" She laughed. "Everything has changed so much so fast that I think I'm still adjusting to it all."

"They love your skanky ass, so get over it." What remained unsaid was if those guys ever harmed a hair on Chloe's head, I'd wreak vengeance the likes of which they would never forget.

"Enough about me, what about you? I saw

those three hotties you went off with last night. If I wasn't already hooked up…"

I would have arm wrestled Chloe for them. "Admit it, you are super jealous I was kidnapped by three werewolves."

"Did you have a good time?"

Admitting the truth meant shattering Chloe's perception that I was a woman of the world, a femme fatale. I wasn't ready for that yet. "We had a howling good time. Even indulged in a little bondage."

My BFF laughed. "You are incorrigible, Brenda."

"I know." Now, if only I were more loveable, then I wouldn't be hitting the singles bars looking for love and coming home alone.

I should get myself a puppy. A real furry one that would love me unconditionally.

It might help me to not pine over the dogs that had not once tried to hump my leg or lick my lips—upper or lower, I wouldn't have cared.

Chapter Four

A few weeks passed, and the werewolves didn't chase me down to give me a nibble, not even a single crotch sniff.

No more demons were sighted.

Not a single feline became possessed—although I had my suspicions about the cat lady on the third floor.

Life returned to normal.

Yay. Did you catch the huge amount of sarcasm in there?

Sighing, I tossed yet another ball of paper at the waste basket and missed. My level of boredom had hit epic heights. Part of it had to do with my best friend being busy with her boyfriends—doing the naked tango and couples dinners and probably shopping for matching shirts.

My spare time lately involved watching a lot of Netflix, trolling social media, cursing at Candy Crush, and eating. Going to work and the grocery store were probably the most exciting things I had going, and of the two, working as part of the secretarial pool had lost its shine.

It didn't take much effort to blame the tedious job—type, type, answer the phone, type some more, and file—but the real truth was that ever since that bit of excitement a few weeks ago with the demon stalking Chloe—the lucky bitch— I'd found myself less than content.

And, no, my doldrums had nothing to do with the three guys I'd met a few weeks ago, who never once tried to call.

Who cared about three jerks who couldn't see what an amazing catch I was? A better catch than any tennis ball, I might add.

Their loss.

Bastards.

However, they had nothing to do with my lack of desire to sort three piles of paper into neat bundles and staple them in the corners.

I wanted more excitement in my life.

No, make that *needed* something to give me a reason to bounce out of bed and have my neighbor below me pound on the ceiling with her cane.

With that thought in mind, I flounced into my BFF's office—at the boring old department of justice building downtown—just before the whistle blew—a real one that I programmed as an alarm on my phone and that I'd filched from *The Flintstones*.

"Life blows hairy donkey balls," I announced, flopping into the chair in front of Chloe's desk.

Her office space wasn't much better than mine. We both had standard-issue government desks with wobbly legs, and drawers that stuck, but where she'd gotten shoved into a tiny cubicle of an office, I was at least out in the secretarial pen.

Think of a bunch of cattle in a square, sitting at desks, pretending to look busy, and you'd have us—with less mooing but more cackling.

Although the us was getting more masculine by the month. The shortage of bodies with a pair of X chromosomes meant more and more women chose to stay home, have babies, and let their husbands—*yes, I said that in plural*—take care of them.

Everyone wanted to do their part rebuilding the world's female population—and cash in on the tax breaks.

Except for me.

Even my BFF Chloe had finally succumbed to a pair of hunks crazy about her, and I imagined it wouldn't be long before she announced she was pregnant with a litter of puppies.

I couldn't wait to present her with a T-shirt that said *Future Dictator* and had an arrow pointing at her belly. Studies said if you raised a kid to think big things, they would do big things.

Which made me wonder what happened to me? Meemaw always told me I'd kick ass in the world if I wasn't afraid to try.

Well, hello, not afraid over here, and yet life kept passing me by.

"What are you thinking? I can hear the gears in your mind churning. That's never a good thing," Chloe said.

"I was imagining you pregnant."

"What?" Good thing Chloe didn't have anything in her mouth. As it was, I practically felt the fine spray of spittle as she shouted, "I'm not pregnant. Nor do I plan to be."

"Are you telling me you're using rubbers every time?"

"Mostly." At my arched brow, she shrugged. "Okay, maybe not so much. But we've been tested. We're clean. And I'm on the pill."

"A human pill," I muttered ominously. "You're sleeping with a vampire and a werewolf. What makes you think they don't have super sperm?" Wearing little capes, bulleting their way toward the egg, determined to save the world by impregnating my friend.

"Can vampires even make babies?" she asked. Her face adopted a slightly horrified expression. "Would a vampire baby suck my blood from the inside?"

Sounded familiar, probably because I saw it in a movie. In reality, while a whole bunch of bogeymen came out of the closet, vampires didn't. Go figure, the one creature everyone kind of believed in didn't want the world to know for sure.

But I knew because Chloe didn't keep secrets from me.

Now if only I were a better friend and she knew the truth about me.

I'm not the hot commodity you think I am. In truth, I was the sad loser friend, the duff who couldn't keep a man.

"Anthony's not a sadistic prick. I doubt he would impregnate you with a life-sucking leech without telling you. But, if it makes you feel better, if you should die from a parasite eating its way out of your stomach, I will avenge you." I kept a stake sharpened under my pillow and a revolver loaded with silver. And, unlike the crew of *The Walking Dead*, I didn't have some tiny little knife that would force me to get close to a zombie. I had a three-foot machete.

When, not *if*, the apocalypse came, I would face it properly armed.

"Thank you, I think." Chloe bit her lower lip. "Perhaps it's time the boys and I chatted about the birds and the bees."

"Why? Let nature take its course and don't worry. If it happens, it will be great. Any kid you birth is bound to be cute. Have you seen the prospective fathers?" I rolled my eyes and laughed.

Any babies born of Chloe and her men would have a cocktail of awesomeness in their veins. And Chloe would have all the support she needed. I could just imagine how much her lovers would mollycoddle her if she carried their future namesake in her tummy.

Lucky bitch. I could only hope to aspire to that kind of awesome devotion. Men tended to be thrown off by my rather upfront nature. They also labeled me aggressive, bossy, demanding, and scary.

Pussies.

But at least they all agreed I was cute before dumping me, which, in turn, forced me to hurt them. Meemaw always said, "If he doesn't see what a treasure you are, then punch him." Literally.

I couldn't pine after a guy who collapsed and cried after I dropped him. None of the men I met could handle me.

None until recently.

Dale didn't fall when I attacked him. An insidious reminder that Dale had barely flinched when I went rabid squirrel on him.

In my defense, he had backup.

One on one, I could take him, all of them.

Could have. Par for the course, I never heard from or saw them again.

"Why do you look so blue?" Chloe asked. "Is it because I've got to miss TGIF tonight?"

Way to remind me. "I can't believe you're ditching an evening of large tropical drinks in unnaturally fluorescent colors adorned with cherries and umbrellas to go see a movie."

"Not just any movie. Anthony is taking me to see the latest *Planet of the Apes* movie." Her hands clapped excitedly, and her eyes shone with delight. Chloe had a thing for cheesy flicks.

"Instead of going tonight, you could go for a matinee tomorrow. It will be less crowded."

"Crowds aren't an issue. Anthony buys the seats all around so no one can sit in them."

"I assume it's because all those yummy heartbeats make him hungry?" I asked.

Chloe's mouth rounded. "Of course not. He just doesn't like people that close to me in public. Especially since he likes to, um, er, you know, during the movie."

"Do what?" I asked innocently. I could easily guess, but it was fun to see my best friend blush and squirm. At least someone was having a good time.

"Things." Said with bright red cheeks.

"Ugh, I can't believe you'd pass on free drinks and dancing for an orgasm in public." There might have been a hint of jealousy on my part in there.

"Guilt-trip me all you like, but now that I'm kind of taken, isn't it false advertising for me to hang out in a singles bar?"

"Oh, please, like some of those guys aren't already hooked up and just looking for an extra piece of action."

"I get enough action. So much action," she cooed, deliberately needling me.

I loved it. About time she found her own inner strength.

Sad as it made me, I was happy to see Chloe entering a new chapter of her life, one that involved less of me. She deserved a chance to build a family, birth a legacy, and I wasn't about to get in her way. A real friend would set me up, though. "So, Anthony, no brother, hunh?" Being an old vampire, he kind of outlived his family.

A shake of her head. "Nope. Sorry. I asked. Just like he doesn't know any other vampires he'd trust you with."

Nice to know he wanted to keep me alive. It wouldn't stop me from staking him if he ever hurt Chloe, though.

"And what about Fido?" Pete and I had an odd relationship. I asked him all kinds of questions, and he got flustered and found reasons to leave. What kind of man didn't have a yes or no answer for, "do you prefer it doggy style?"

Chloe shrugged. "I bugged him, but Pete

says all the guys he knows are dogs."

Wolves, but no point in quibbling. I'd met some of his friends, and apparently, I wasn't their version of an irresistible Scooby snack.

"Well, surely you know someone." For a moment, my desperation came through, and I hoped she didn't hear it. *I'm supposed to have my shit together. Don't lose it now.*

"I wish I knew someone so we could double date."

"By double date, I am going to assume we're not swapping keys."

It took Chloe a moment. "Brenda! We are not swapping boyfriends."

"You say that now, but wait until you see my next one…"

"Only one? Don't tell me you're going to go old school."

For some reason, I thought of a trio of men I wouldn't mind calling my own.

However, since I couldn't snare one, what hope did I have of nabbing three?

"Speaking of dudes I can date, what about the guy who just left?"

"You mean my client, Mr. Peabody?" Chloe squeaked his name. "Did you not see the handcuffs?"

"A little bondage never hurt anyone." Unless they tied up a girl and didn't put out. "So, is he single?"

"Brenda, don't even kid like that. You can do much better than that."

No, apparently I couldn't. But even I

should have standards.

While looks weren't everything, Mr. Peabody lacked any pretty features and any kind of suave confidence. A gangly fellow with rounded shoulders, a sallow complexion, and a few ginger strands combed over a shiny white pate.

A guy with swagger could overcome many physical issues. Bad hair, annoying laugh, pot belly, bad taste in movies, but a dude who lacked looks and attitude?

I'd put out an ad in the paper first.

Desperate chick needs a man, preferably one who doesn't understand English.

"What was he in here for? Peeping Tom?" He looked the creepy type to grip a windowsill and stare over the ledge. "Wearing a trench coat and flashing his junk?" Put it away. No one wanted to see that.

"Actually, it's more fucked up than that. Mr. Peabody is accused of trying to set his house on fire, while his family was sleeping inside."

"Doesn't sound too fucked up to me. Arsonist and murderer. Happens all the time." As a secretary for the state's legal department, stuff came across my desk all the time. The most common being crimes of passion—if I can't have you, no one can. Closely followed by cases of the crazy-voices-made-me-do-it variety.

After a while, you became numb to it. Cynical about the evil of mankind. It was probably why I had less of a problem with Chloe's animal boyfriends than she had at first. I saw the reports on monsters every day, and they were human.

Chloe tapped the folder sitting atop her desk. "Mr. Peabody is actually being charged with attempted murder. But I've requested a mental evaluation. They're taking him over to the institution right now. Either Peabody has a few screws loose, or there is something truly whacked out happening at his house."

"Whacked out how? What's he claiming?"

"Peabody claims his house is alive and that it possessed his family." Chloe swirled a finger alongside her head in a universal nutjob sign.

"His house is haunted?" Interest piqued, I sat up.

"Haunted. Possessed. Evil." Chloe shrugged. "Peabody says he tried getting it exorcised. It failed."

More and more interesting. "Did the priest start speaking in strange tongues? Spewing ectoplasmic vomit?"

"No idea. No one knows what happened, so Mr. Peabody is being investigated for the cleric's disappearance as well."

"That scrawny dude killed a priest?"

"He claims the house ate him. Then turned his family against him, which is why Peabody tried to burn the house down. He wanted to cleanse them with fire."

"Dude, that is like an epic case."

"Epic if it were true. I haven't verified any of his claims yet. Which is why we're having him evaluated."

"If it does turn out he's crazy, is he going to have to stay in the loony bin?"

"Awhile, but worst part is"—Chloe leaned forward and lowered her voice—"I kind of believe him. Which is why I'm sending a copy of the case over to TDCM."

"Oooooh." For those that never ran into them before, TDCM stood for the Thaumaturgic Department for the Concealment of Magic. A secret investigative organization run by none other than wizards. Most humans didn't know the TDCM existed.

But I was special.

And bored.

I leaned forward and slapped my hands on the desk. "Let me in on it."

"What?"

"Please, Chloe. I am tired of typing up boring briefs and filing stupid paper that's just going to be shredded in a few years."

"But that's what your job is. You're not a cop."

"Neither is Frederick"—the office brown nose—"and he's always running around for you guys, tracking down shit. Plus, he's human."

"So are you."

"I am pretty sure I was a mermaid in another life, which means I should be the one working on this case, not Frederick. He doesn't know what to look for. You know he'll ignore anything magical that he comes across."

"Valid point." Chloe's lips twisted as she mused over my argument.

I prodded some more. "With my open mind, I'm more likely to see stuff, things that might prove your client innocent."

"The wizards can probably find magic stuff more easily than you," Chloe said gently.

"Maybe. But you need an impartial set of eyes and ears. Who better than me? You know I'll tell you the truth. Plus, look at all the experience I have."

"You've never dealt with a haunted house or possession before." Chloe paused. "Have you?"

"No, but I've seen all the *Amityville* movies and the knock-offs. I can handle a spooky house. I *need* this." Needed to do something that excited me.

"But it sounds dangerous. Didn't you hear what Peabody claimed happened to the priest? The house ate him."

I'd heard. Could anyone see the giddiness inside? "The real question is, did the priest enjoy it?"

"Brenda!"

"What?" I shrugged, a less than innocent expression on my face. "It's a valid question. After all, the priest probably never gets any action. Holy vows and all that shit. Who's to say he's not having a grand ol' time inside those walls?"

"You are one sick puppy, Brenda."

"More like a bored and caged songbird who needs to fly free!" I flung out my arms and rapped my knuckles off a filing cabinet.

Damned small space.

"Let me do this," I pleaded.

Chloe tapped a nail on the desk. "I am kind of swamped, and given Mr. Peabody is my client, I should keep an eye on what transpires. Both with the TDCM and the actual police department."

"What? I could be working with cops?" My interest took off running and leaping. It expended itself in a bounce that caused the old chair I was sitting in to creak alarmingly. "Please, Chloe. Let me handle this."

"If I do, you have to promise you won't go to that house by yourself, just in case any of it is true."

"If you insist, I'll surround myself with at least a pair of men in uniform before going over to the house." Oh, the hardship of being guarded by cops. The horror.

The possibilities…

The file slid across the desk, not so thick, yet filled with real crime scene notes, witness statements, all kinds of yummy stuff.

"You'll have to do this on top of your regular stuff. You know how Craig is about losing a secretary for what he calls 'unnecessary extras.' But I will make sure you get paid overtime."

Could this deal get any better?

Dye my hair red, throw me in a purple mini dress, and call me Daphne. I was going to crack this case.

Chapter Five

Determined to make Chloe proud of me, and finally excited about something in my life, I decided to go about this job intelligently.

Despite my intense desire to rush off to see if the house would try and eat me without taking me on an expensive date first, I stopped and came up with a concise plan of action.

First things first, I chose to gather more information. Only a few witness statements padded the folder. One each from Peabody's wife and two kids. Another by the first officers to arrive on the scene, and then Mr. Peabody himself.

Guess whose was the most interesting?

Really, if you thought about it, what better person to begin this investigation with than the culprit himself, Mr. Peabody?

Alfred Dickson Peabody, which, for some reason, made me giggle. What were his parents thinking?

With my credentials in place—legal assistant to the defense attorney in charge of Mr. Peabody's case, proven by the stack of business cards I filched from Chloe's desk—the following morning, bright and early, I was allowed through the gates to the loony bin.

Ahem, the Lupium Psychiatric Evaluation Center—for the truly crazy.

Making it through the heavy-duty gate with barbed wire at the top, I parked in front of the massive building. When the gentleman in the white coat and matching pants ran out the front to greet me with a shouted, "You can't park there," I handed him my keys.

He gaped, and I patted his cheek and said, "Be a dear and park it in the shade so it doesn't get too hot." I didn't figure I'd be long. An hour at most, less if Mr. Peabody was too busy catching mental butterflies to talk to me.

My heels clicked as I strode through the heavy doors. In my role as awesome assistant, I'd chosen to wear all red. Short red jacket over a red blouse, with a red pencil skirt and matching red shoes.

The lipstick? A shade of red called Blow Me. Which, if you asked me, was kind of backwards. Shouldn't it be called Blow You?

The male nurse manning the reception eyed me, utterly speechless. I could see he was quite taken by my appearance.

Despite knowing it might stun him into incoherence, I smiled as I introduced myself. "Brenda Jane Whittaker, here to see Mr. Peabody."

"You can't see him looking like that."

"Like what?" I looked down at myself before meeting his gaze. "I can't help how pretty I am. It's how I was born." Well, not exactly, but the laser eye surgery, dermatological treatments, and braces I'd worn for about five years weren't something the receptionist needed to know about.

"I was talking about the color you're wearing. Red." He shook his head. "Didn't anyone tell you that Mr. Peabody can't stand it? It sets him off."

"Oops. I must have missed that part." I batted my lashes. Naughty me, I *had* read that tidbit in the report and thought to use it to my advantage. Throw the lunatic off his meds and get him to spill some secrets.

The receptionist, with a name tag saying *Oscar*, frowned. "I'm sorry, ma'am, but you'll have to come back when you're more suitably attired."

Ma'am? Please don't tell me I'd finally migrated from the Miss age group.

Am I truly so old? Nah, because Oscar was surely older than me.

Oscar was also in my way.

"You expect me to leave without doing my job?" I slapped a hand to my chest. "My boss will kill me."

Actually, my boss would probably sigh and wonder why she'd given me this case to work.

"I have rules I have to follow."

"And here I would have thought you were a man who thought outside the box." I batted my lashes.

I had no shame. I'd flirt with anything, even this man wearing a ring on his finger.

His lips pursed. "Do you have a spare set of clothes?"

I shook my head. "Couldn't you loan me a coat or something to wear over my ensemble? I could leave the shoes here at your desk."

A little more batting of my eyes, a tissue to wipe my lips, and an offer to let him borrow my shoes while I talked to Mr. Peabody—hoping Oscar wouldn't stretch them too badly—meant a few minutes later, I was wrapped in a huge doctor's coat and being led barefoot down a sterile, gray hall.

Every single door we passed worked by fingerprint scan. No cards or keys. It made me wonder how anyone would escape.

And why such strict security? These were people with mental issues. Not serial killers.

Or were they? I hadn't yet seen Mr. Peabody's garden. I wondered how his flowers grew.

I couldn't remember if it was a movie or documentary that told me decomposing bodies made the best fertilizer. But if I saw an unusually lush lawn or plants when I did visit his home, I planned to dig.

The room I entered closely resembled my idea of an asylum common area. I almost clapped my hands in delight. The vast room had a wall of windows, each one caged by metal bars, and a tiled floor in a green-and-white-checkered pattern, spanning a good twenty by thirty feet at least. A good-sized space.

The room appeared divided into different areas of interest from a comfy side with a couch and chairs, to a section with tables and plastic chairs—chained to the floor, spoiling any possible fight. Board games and cards littered the tabletops.

A large desk holding a partially completed puzzle and loose pieces sat by a window. In another corner, an area with a few easels and stools for the artistically inclined.

I rather liked the piece of art sketched in dark charcoal of a stick man holding a head dripping blue and green.

The communal area held at least a dozen or more patients, all of them wearing plain garments, track suits for the most part, although a few did wander around in robes. The hues ranged from a light green, pale yellow, or white to the most common gray with hints of past color.

Over by a drawing easel, Mr. Peabody wore a tracksuit, the loose material bulking his slim frame. He leaned forward, sketching furiously, and I snuck up behind him to take a peek.

"Dude, are those eyes?" Jumping from the canvas, the surface streaked and whorled in black, he'd drawn two giant yellow orbs.

"The darkness watches," he muttered aloud.

"Watches what? Prime time? CNN? *Riverdale*?" My new addiction, mostly because of a certain hottie with red hair.

"He watches for the sign."

"Sign of what? Are we talking candle in the window? Phase of the moon?" I hated it when people only uttered half an answer, especially when I was eavesdropping. How was I supposed to know when Ted claimed he was cheating that it wasn't on his boyfriend Brian in accounting but on his diet?

I perched on a stool alongside Mr. Peabody.

"Hey, Mr. Peabody, I'm Brenda." I held out my hand, which went ignored, but I excused him the poor manners. After all, he was crazy.

Tucking my hands in my lap, I resisted the urge to grab a crayon and give the eyes in his drawing long and luscious eyelashes.

"You're probably wondering why I'm here. I'm helping Chloe with your case." When he didn't reply, I slapped myself, then hoped no one had seen it lest they think I was nuts, too. "I guess you don't know her by her first name. I work for Ms. Bailey, your lawyer."

"Has she napalmed the house yet?" He craned his head to ask me, and I got the full force of Peabody's gaze.

Washed-out blue eyes that didn't quite focus on me or anything else in this reality, I'd wager. Under the fluorescent lights, his pallid skin appeared gray, and his teeth yellow.

"About the house, we have some questions first before we demolish the place. Let's start at the beginning."

"More questions?" Peabody sighed as he turned the paper he'd drawn on over the top and prepared to work on a new masterpiece. "If you must."

Easy peasy. I pulled out my notepad to take notes. "When exactly did you move into your house?"

"Fifteen years ago. We bought it just before the birth of our son. Marcus. He plays football, you know."

I didn't know. I didn't care. But I played

nice. "According to the bank, you still owe about twenty years on the mortgage."

"We refinanced."

I made a noise as I scribbled. "What do you do for work?"

"I'm a manager for a shoe store."

"Appalling." Not the job, the fact that a man who worked in a shoe store now had to wear paper slippers. "Do you like your job?"

"What does that have to do with my evil house?"

"Nothing, but now I feel like I should ask, was your house always evil?"

His lips pursed. "Like I told Ms. Bailey, the incidents only started about two months ago."

"What kinds of incidents? What was the first thing you noticed?"

"The cockroaches in the basement."

Gross, but not exactly supernatural. "Did you call an exterminator?"

"I did. And we solved that problem, only to run into another. A crack appeared."

"A crack leading to a Hell dimension?"

"No, a crack in the foundation. It cost me almost ten grand to get it fixed." Mr. Peabody frowned. "And then they refused to repair it under warranty when the crack reappeared less than two weeks later. Claimed my house wasn't sitting on a solid foundation."

"Because you're actually sitting atop an ancient graveyard?"

"What?" His eyes widened. "No. The house was built atop a marsh that they filled in. Not very well, I might add. It's slowly sinking. But that's not why the lights started flickering."

The more Mr. Peabody talked, the more I wondered if Chloe had it wrong. Sounded like an old house with problems.

"Nothing an electrician couldn't fix. I have to say, you're disappointing me so far." I tucked my hands over my notepad.

"You think I'm crazy. All of you do." He stared around suspiciously. "But I'm not. I knew there was something evil going on when stuff started disappearing."

"What disappeared? Family pet? Small child?"

"No, nothing like that. Jewelry. Electronics. "

Like I hadn't heard that before. "Does your son do drugs?" I didn't sugarcoat it. Parents in denial needed a wake-up call.

"If you're suggesting Marcus pawned our things, then you're wrong. My son wasn't behind it. And even he wouldn't have been able to make our dining room set disappear in the middle of the night."

I doubted very many drug dealers would take bulky furniture in payment. Then again... "Where do think the stuff went?"

Thin shoulders lifted and fell. "Who knows, I never saw any of it again. When I woke one morning to find all the carpeting gone, I knew it was time to get some help."

Disappearing carpets? Now we were talking. "That's when you called the priest."

"No, I invested in cameras. When they failed to record anything, even the night the stove disappeared—"

"Hold on a second. Surely your equipment saw something."

He shook his head. "The videos showed the cameras started recording fine, then at one point during the night, the recordings went blank."

"Like fuzzy snow blank or the kind that turns into a little girl crawling out of a well coming for you?" That spooky movie was why I'd taken a hammer to my VHS player and all my tapes. The vodka and the match were what got me a visit from those cute firemen.

"The video feed was blank. Every single one of them. That's when I called the priest."

Finally, the meaty part of his tale. "What kind of priest?"

He blinked. "Excuse me?"

"What kind? Christian, Buddhist, Jewish, Muslim… I mean, there's like a shit-ton of choices these days when it comes to religion."

"I called the Catholic Church, as they are usually the most equipped to deal with these kinds of evil hauntings."

"So the priest arrived, and then what? He walked through the front door, and the house gulped him down?"

A shake of his head.

"He threw around some holy water, and the floor opened up to swallow him?"

An irritated crease of his brow and a sharp, "No!"

My imagination had plenty more to offer. "He leaned against a wall, and whoops, got sucked in?"

"I don't know. I didn't see what happened. All I know is he went into the house and never came out."

That was Peabody's proof? Thin even by my low standards. "So you don't actually know for sure the house ate him?"

"What else could have happened?"

"Maybe he decided a change of career was in order, but he didn't want to deal with the paperwork, so he sneaked out your back door, switching out his clothes on the way, hopped the fence, and hitched a ride to Texas to become a cowboy."

Mr. Peabody blinked. Amazed at the possibility he'd overlooked.

"And they think I'm crazy," he muttered.

"Speaking of crazy, according to the police report and what you told my boss, you have this theory your family is possessed."

"It's not a theory. They are possessed." He practically spat the word, and some of the insanity began to creep back into his gaze.

"What makes you think they're being ridden by a spectral parasite? Are they glowing in the dark? Measuring sub-human body temperature? Floating off the floor? Crawling out of wells?" I was on a roll, and Mr. Peabody just kept shaking his head. "Crab-walking across ceilings? Spinning their heads? Spewing wasps from their mouth?"

"No. No. And no." He got quite loud.

How rude. I was simply trying to get to the truth.

"If there were no outward signs, then how did you know they were possessed?"

"Because they claimed to not see a thing."

I blinked a few times as I digested this. "What do you mean they didn't see a thing?"

"I mean, they claimed the dining room set was still there. That nothing was missing. They even claimed the priest never came to our house. Obviously, their minds are being manipulated."

"Obviously." I snapped my notebook shut and tucked my crayon in the coat pocket—because the receptionist had confiscated my lovely ballpoint pen. Apparently, it could be used as a weapon. I kind of wanted it right now to stab myself with for having wasted a lovely Saturday morning.

I rose from my perch.

"Where are you going?" he cried.

"Away. I can see you're exactly where you should be. I should have talked to your family first."

"Stay away from them. They're dangerous. Evil."

"They're not the ones locked up in here."

"You have to believe me. It's the house. It's behind everything. You need to burn it down. All of it."

"By all of it, are you including your supposedly possessed family?"

At that, his face crumpled. "No. Spare them. Maybe if the house is gone, they'll return to themselves."

Or maybe with crazy Daddy gone, they'd get a chance at a normal life.

Despite what Chloe thought, I doubted Mr. Peabody's house was haunted. The more likely scenario was that the home found itself in need of major renovation, and Peabody snapped when he found out his wife had cheated on him with the general contractor.

My job done here, I stood, and because I couldn't help my curiosity, I stripped off the coat, revealing my splendid red outfit.

A hush fell over the room. A seriously awesome quiet as everyone admired my sleek style.

Peabody's eyes grew huge. So big I thought they might fall out of his face. His mouth opened so wide I wondered if his jaw was double hinged.

The screaming started, a fire engine wail pouring from his gaping mouth.

No big deal. I'd made men scream before.

What had me gaping was the fact that Mr. Peabody floated off the floor!

Chapter Six

There are many things a girl should do when confronted with a man who kept screaming without taking a breath as he floated about two feet off the floor.

Pretty sure clapping wasn't one of them.

Still, it was a pretty epic moment. I couldn't help but stare and slap my hands together. I did, however, restrain myself from shouting, "Bravo" and "About time."

And the show wasn't done!

Peabody's entire body arched, bowing to the point that things snapped, crackled, and popped. The entire room vibrated, and a strange breeze brushed past my cheek, lifting my hair and bringing a sulfuric stench. The asylum ventilation system needed some maintenance.

"You." A finger pointed.

"Me?" I mouthed, bringing my hands to my chest.

"You smell tasty." His head cocked, and he licked his lips.

"Thank you." I couldn't recall the name of the perfume, but it didn't cost me much from the vendor on the street.

"Good enough to eat."

Finally, someone paying me attention. Alas, I didn't find myself interested. "Thanks, but no thanks. I draw the line at married dudes in asylums."

"Silence!"

The proclamation came with a punch of air that hit me and carried me across the room to smack into something hard.

"Oomph," said the wall, who stopped my flight. It also grabbed and held me. Not the wall, but someone.

Someone who smelled like Old Spice.

A man.

But not just any man. One that I knew.

Peeking over my shoulder, I managed a smile at Mike. "Well, if isn't Mr. Grumpy. Fancy meeting you he-r-r-e." The word screeched out of me as the fist of air grabbed me and dragged me away from Mike to the center of the room, where it held me suspended.

Despite what you might think, an air mattress really wasn't as comfortable as memory foam. I also didn't care for the floor show, which, in this case, was a ceiling show.

Mr. Peabody might not have seen his family crabbing across the ceiling, but he certainly could. Looking rather disjointed, he moved, defying gravity while I gaped.

Mostly in excitement because, hot damn, Peabody had actually told the truth. Kind of. He was the one possessed!

Oh, and his crazy haunted ass was after me, which sounded more fun in theory than reality.

"Fee, fi, fo, fum, I smell some blood."

It didn't rhyme at the end, but I got the gist. It wasn't good for me.

"Strip!" a man yelled.

Finally, Mike showed an interest in me. A little bit too late.

"Sorry, Grumpy, but I don't think now's the time to get intimately acquainted."

Peabody scuttled closer, and it was shiver-inducing. Despite what the movies showed, in this case, not even a certain red and blue spider costume would make him hot.

Peabody, his eyes completely white, stared at me. A tongue, fat and purple, whipped out to lick his stretched lips. As drool began to pool from Peabody, I cringed.

Spit and other bodily fluids should only be seen during sex.

"Shut up for once and listen to me," Mike said from somewhere below me. "Red sets him off. Try removing it. Maybe that will help veer his attention."

Figured Mike asked me to get naked for a practical reason and not a carnal one.

Still, his idea had merit.

I began to strip, shrugging off my coat, with Mike muttering, "Can't you undress faster?"

"Maybe if I had some help," I grumbled, giving up on the buttons for my blouse and yanking, popping them with little pings.

The blouse came off and fluttered down, and I noted Peabody's gaze bouncing between the tossed shirt and me. More specifically, what I wore below the waist.

Before I could tackle my skirt, Peabody hovered over me, his head bent at a freakishly inhuman angle.

"Lunch time," he sang.

Fuck the horror movies and being brave.

I screamed like a girl, not as good as Jamie Lee Curtis in *Prom Night*, but it was close.

Peabody began to drop, floating closer and closer.

I tried to swim away from him, but I couldn't get traction in midair.

"Yummy, yummy, in my tummy." Peabody's voice sang the ditty over and over.

I heard the screech of metal on the floor. A moment later, someone grabbed my arm and yanked. The air fist holding me aloft popped, and I was pulled into the arms of a man standing on a chair.

A chair that fell over with our combined weight so that I tumbled atop my rescuer.

Mike.

I smiled. "Hey, good looking, what's cooking?"

"Move!" he yelled before tossing me to the side.

I rolled a few times before coming to a stop. Pushing myself up on my elbows, I peeked and saw Mike, dressed in plain trousers and a white shirt grappling with Peabody.

Actually, it was less wrestling and more holding Peabody still. The crazy man's eyes were fixated on me. Not my almost naked boobs in their demi-cup bra but my bottom half.

My red skirt.

I scrambled to my feet and did a shimmy. My hands trembled as I pushed at my skirt, dropping the red fabric in a puddle on the floor then dashing away from it.

Mr. Peabody burst free from Mike and leaped at the skirt, pouncing on it and tearing it to shreds.

Only when he'd reduced it back to the thread it began life as did he stop. Scooting over to his easel, Peabody perched on it, a vulture with a black crayon drawing big, angry circles.

As for me, I stood in my matching underwear—slutty black lace, not red—the focus of everyone's attention.

Including Mike's.

But his gaze didn't admire. Not according to the giant scowl on his face and his barked, "Put this on and come with me."

Mike Interlude

What the fuck is she doing here?

When the commotion started, people running down the hall yelling, an alarm going off, Mike had immediately headed to the common room following the foot traffic. What he'd not expected to see, or get hit with, the moment he walked in the door was an itty-bitty woman wearing red.

The red clothes were gone now, and he'd seen more than he needed.

More than he could forget.

"Who the hell let you in here?" he snapped, his grip tight on Brenda's arm, the fabric of the white coat he'd forced on her keeping him from touching skin.

Too late to save him. The vision of her standing in only her panties and bra had burnt itself on his retinas.

"I am here on business."

"What kind of business? The red flag waving in front of a rabid bull?"

"Where is all this hate for red coming from?" Brenda yanked her arm from his grip and glared at him. "I looked very nice."

"You did. And very red, which is what sets

off the spirit inside Peabody."

Her expression went from angry to excited. "So he is the one possessed."

"Very. But we've managed to keep it mostly dormant."

Her lips pushed out into a pout. "That's no fun. How are you supposed to get answers then?"

"Maybe by ensuring he's restrained first." Mike pushed open the door to his office and ushered her in. Only when he slammed it shut did he whirl and then manhandle her until her back pressed against the wall.

"Ooh, Grumpy. I never expected this kind of reaction from you."

He hadn't either. For some reason, the sight and scent of Brenda did things to him. Carnal things he didn't like.

"What are you really doing here?"

"I told you, I had business."

"Bullshit. The real reason." Because no one in their right mind would send her to question Peabody. Then again, no one knew just how fucked up Peabody was.

"Would you believe me if I said I came to see you?" She batted her lashes.

He didn't buy it for a second.

"What do you want with Mr. Peabody?"

"I think the better question, Grumpy, is why are you here? Did your angry view of the world finally get you locked up for observation? Did you lose your favorite chew toy and go into a puppy depression?"

"Did your mother drop you on your head

as a child?" he snarled in her face.

"I had no mother."

Prick. The sound of his anger deflated at her little words.

"That's no excuse." He moved away from Brenda and flopped into his chair behind the desk.

She peeked around, completely unfazed by the fact that a possessed man had tried to attack her. He, on the other hand, still rode high on adrenaline.

"Who's office is this?" she asked. "Shrink? The guy who doles out drugs. The man who gives people dolls and asks them to show where they were touched?"

How about the office of a man who needed a good slap for some of the thoughts running through his mind?

"The office is mine," he stated.

"They give patients offices?" Her nose wrinkled as she looked around.

He fought an urge to scrounge for drugs. "I'm not a patient. I work here. As a doctor." Of sorts. The Lycium Institute catered only to the non-humans. Those that needed care from someone who understood them and knew how to contain them.

"A doctor? Do you have any idea how hot that makes you?" She stood there, hair disheveled, wearing a coat—with hardly anything underneath—tapping her chin with a finger.

Did she have any idea how sexy that made her?

If he liked humans.

And even if he did, he'd choose to like a sane one, not a crazy Thumbelina-sized vixen who threw herself into danger and didn't seem to care.

"Why were you talking to Mr. Peabody?"

"Are you jealous?" She sat primly in the seat across from him, crossing her legs, forcing the seam in the coat to fall open, revealing lots of bare thigh.

He averted his gaze.

"If you're implying that I'm jealous that he tried to kill you instead of me, then no, not particularly. However, as his physician, I am supposed to be in charge of who speaks to him."

"What a lucky chance I ran into you then because he's part of my job."

"What job? I thought you were a secretary." And yes, he did sneer.

"I am, but Chloe asked me to help her out on account that she's so busy, especially now with the two boyfriends. Not that I'm not busy, too," Brenda hastened to add.

"So busy you decided to hit the asylum for a Saturday-morning visit."

"I wouldn't cast any stones there, Grumpy. You're here, too."

"Because they pay me."

"Who says I'm not getting paid?"

"You work for the government. They aren't known to be generous with their overtime hours."

"Good point." She slouched, but not for long.

Nothing ever seemed to keep her spirits down. Just like nothing would keep his dick down.

He'd sat down behind the cover of his desk for a reason.

"So, what can you tell me about Mr. Peabody?" She leaned forward, and her jacket gaped. Being a man—and part wolf—he couldn't help but look.

It was a prime directive. He liked what he saw.

A little too much.

He focused on her question. "I can't tell you anything about Mr. Peabody because of doctor-patient privilege."

"Even if I say pretty please?" She batted her lashes.

"No."

"But I'm working on his defense case."

"And I'm working to keep him from killing himself or others. Guess what trumps you?"

"You're impeding justice." She jumped to her feet and slammed her hands on his desk.

"And you're trouble. I don't want you coming back here."

"I might have to if I have more questions."

"Then visit a library."

"You can't stop me from finding out the truth," she threatened, leaning over his desk.

The coat gaped wider, showing off the vale between her breasts, tempting him…

I could lick a path down to those tiny little panties and…

He half rose to meet her until they were almost nose-to-nose before growling, "Oh, yes I can stop you." He had to stop her. Had to make her leave. This attraction he had for her was madness.

"Bet you can't stop this."

Before he could guess her intent, she'd grabbed him by the hair and yanked him close.

Her lips, soft and tasting faintly of lipstick, pressed against his.

Shocked, he couldn't move as her mouth slanted over his, nibbling and sucking. Teasing him with soft kisses.

The tip of her tongue parted the seam of his mouth, and he might have rumbled as she deepened the caress. Brenda somehow ended up atop the desk, on her knees, her arms twined around his neck.

And his hands?

They slid inside the coat, encountering soft skin, and lush curves.

Pure madness.

Unadulterated pleasure that made him want to howl and stamp a foot.

He couldn't help but touch her, cup the fullness of her ass, let his tongue dance with hers in a frantic embrace that saw him breathing hard.

Sanity returned for a moment.

He pulled away. "We can't do this."

"Yes, we can." She cupped his face. "Kiss me."

An order he knew he should ignore. Instead, he dove onto her mouth.

With her already mostly naked, it was all too easy for him to slide a hand under the elastic of her panties, to reach in and cup her mound.

To touch her.

Feel her wetness. Her heat. Her desire.

...*for me.*

He couldn't help but stroke her, slide a finger back and forth across her wet slit, hearing her moan as he caressed.

A part of him knew what they did was wrong.

He couldn't have explained why or how it was wrong, though. How could it be wrong when it felt so good?

He dipped a finger into her damp sex, feeling the molten, wet heat, the muscles of her channel squeezing him.

He inserted a second finger, and her mouth left his to tease the lobe of his ear, her voice whispering a husky, "Yes, yes."

Yes, this was how it should be. His fingers pumping in and out of her, thrusting and pushing, her body riding them with wild abandon until, with a small cry, she came, the sweet ripple of her orgasm squeezing his fingers so tightly.

How would it feel to sink his cock into that blessed heat?

Before he could remove all the garments standing in their way, she pushed away.

"Goodness, Grumpy, that was an unexpected delight." Her smile and flushed cheeks bemused him.

Perhaps that was why he couldn't react when she slid off his desk and tugged the coat closed while moving to the door.

He gaped at her. "Where are you going?"

They weren't done. His throbbing cock screamed for relief.

"Weren't you the one who said I should go and never come back?"

"Yes, but that was before…" Before he'd lost his mind. Before he'd touched her.

Before he'd made her come on his fingers.

"Is this your way of asking for a thank you?" She cocked her head. "Thank you."

"That's it?" What he really wanted to scream was, *what about me?*

"I wouldn't want to get you in trouble at work. Tell you what, when you're done for the day, if you want, give me a call or pop by my place."

"I'm busy."

"Whatever. Your loss." Her gaze dipped down, and she couldn't miss seeing the erection tenting his slacks. Looking back at him, she winked before sashaying out the door.

Meanwhile, he slumped back into his chair.

What the fuck just happened?

I just finger fucked Brenda. A woman who was off-limits. A woman he didn't even like.

Perhaps Peabody's possession was contagious.

Chapter Seven

My lips and body couldn't stop tingling, and it wasn't just because of the sushi I had for lunch—an interesting experience seeing as how I walked in wearing a doctor's coat, red heels, and fresh lipstick. I needed food to help me process what had happened with Mike.

I'd kissed him, and he finger fucked me to Heaven.

He would have done more, too, but I wanted to think I was getting wiser. Sure, sex on his desk would have been epic. But what about afterwards?

Would he have zipped up and coldly told me to go? By leaving on my own terms, the ball was now in his court. If he truly wanted more of me, then he'd have to come and find me.

Bold. Kind of scary. Because now I'd have to play the waiting game to see if he was interested.

In the meantime, while I waited for him to track me down like a dog after a thrown stick, I went into full-on sleuth mode.

I had a mystery to solve, one involving spirits and shit. Which reminded me, I needed to look into becoming ordained. If I was going to be dealing with crazy, possessed people, then I should have some kind of religion backing me.

After lunch, eaten in my underwear on my living room floor while watching *Poltergeist* at 2X speed—brushing up on my knowledge—I took a quick shower before I dressed in my Norma Louise Bates best. If you've never watched *Bates Motel*, the story of how young Norman got his psycho on, then you're missing out.

As to my outfit... Baby-blue dress with a full skirt, fitted bodice, a lacy sweater, and sensible brown pumps. I fluffed my hair, adjusted the girls, and left my place, ready to tackle the next part of my fact-finding mission.

Having interviewed Mr. Peabody, I found myself full of more questions than ever. Was Mr. Peabody the only victim of possession? Had his wife and kids also been taken over?

Only one way to find out. I needed to visit the family.

But I kind of promised I wouldn't go to that house alone.

Silly assurance really because everyone knew bad shit happened at night. Besides, Peabody was the cuckoo one. I would be safe. But just in case I wasn't, I set up a delayed text for my BFF. A kind of "here's where to look for the body if I go missing" type of thing.

Having done the responsible thing, I turned to the folder Chloe had on Peabody—which I took pictures of because the office had a thing about active files leaving the building. It, of course, had their address and the basics.

Peabody was married, his wife one Margaret

Ann Peabody, age thirty-six. According to the grainy DMV image, she possessed a round face framed with mousy brown hair. A dull expression.

For the kids, Marcus and Melinda, all I had were ages. Fifteen and thirteen.

Horrible years. That was the span of time when I wore the headgear almost twenty-four-seven. Every morning, I set off the metal detector at school. In the end, I didn't mind. It allowed me to smuggle a knife in with me. It came in handy when I had to threaten to cut off Gordon's nuts. Stupid jerk kept calling me Metal Head and asked if my boyfriend, the toaster, had dumped me yet. Gordon said it one time too many, and I might have snapped.

The boys had a much healthier respect for me after the knife incident. When all the shit came off, and the ugly duckling turned into a swan—with attitude—Gordon even tried to get in my pants. The ultimate revenge? I did his best friend instead and told the biggest gossip in school that Gordon had a tiny penis.

My GPS announced, "You have arrived at your destination." What it didn't tell me was to brace myself for disappointment.

Slowing to a stop in front of the house, I double-checked the address—999 Cloven Hoof Lane.

Right place, but massive letdown.

The house that I'd imagined, sitting atop a hill surrounded by a rusted fence sporting turrets—because, hello, haunted houses had turrets—turned out to be a vinyl-sided, split-level in suburbia.

To compound my deflation, it even had a white picket fence and a rosebush—not currently budding, not even with dead, black petals—out front.

This was the evil abode that supposedly possessed Mr. Peabody?

It explained his sense of style.

Hopping out of my truck with my satchel purse hung over my shoulder, I felt ready to face anything. I'd brought some tools to scare the nails out of any haunted house—hammer, pry bar, and a small jar of plaster. If you asked me, many an evil incursion could have been stopped if the homeowners just damn well filled in that crack.

I'd also brought a can of air freshener with me in case the priest hadn't agreed with the house's digestive system.

Funny how I didn't have a problem believing Mr. Peabody's story now, not after what had happened at the asylum.

I sauntered to the front door, clipboard tucked under my arm, cardigan over my shoulders because nothing screamed harmless lady collecting information more than a sweater and sensible shoes.

Knocking on the bright red door—could it be the cause behind Mr. Peabody's aversion?—I stepped back and did my best to look innocent.

I don't know how well I succeeded, given my lips kept pulling into a grin.

Mike liked me.

Kind of.

And I was helping to solve an attempted

murder case.

Life didn't suck, and I couldn't help being happy about it.

The door opened, and expecting the miasma of death or, at the very least, dust and mold, the disappointment proved very real when the scent of freshly baked cookies wafted out.

Mmmm. Cookies.

I blinked at the woman standing just inside the door. "Mrs. Peabody?" I queried. She didn't resemble the image I'd seen at all.

Unlike the dowdy woman in the picture, this woman held herself straight. Sleek brown hair fell in waves over her shoulders. Her bright eyes were perfectly outlined, her lip gloss very discreet.

As for her clothes, she took my Norma Louise Bates and raised it to a June Cleaver with pearls.

Damn.

"Can I help you?" she asked in a lovely modulated voice.

This couldn't be Peabody's wife. The guy I saw would never have won the heart or hand of this gorgeous, sophisticated lady.

Then again, I hadn't seen what he hid in his pants. Must be quite the schlong, given not only was his wife hot but there was also only one Mr. Peabody. A couple that opted to pay higher taxes rather than bring another man into their home was unusual these days.

The mystery deepened.

A bright smile pulled at my lips. "Hello, Mrs. Peabody, I'm here on behalf of the insurance company."

"And which company would that be?"

Being a secretary meant I saw more information than people imagined, such as names of companies, legal treatises, plus how things were managed. Things like say…a husband being incarcerated for insanity.

Someone had to pay for it, and it sure as hell wouldn't be the state.

"Bates Insurance." I held out my hand.

The woman stared at it before shaking, her grip firm and not the least bit sweaty.

Not nervous at all.

"How can I help you, Miss…" She trailed off.

"Letecia Peterson." I'd gone to school with her. Hated her guts because she was naturally pretty, but she came in handy now.

"I'm not sure why you're here, Ms. Peterson. I already spoke to someone on the phone."

"Yes, but we still had a few questions, so they sent me out to find some answers."

"On a Saturday?"

"Insurance is a twenty-four-seven job, ma'am. May I come in?"

For a moment, she paused as if someone had pressed a button. Her expression went blank, her lips remained parted, her eyes unfocused, then she returned to reality.

"Of course, where are my manners? Come in," she said with a titter.

A giggle that marched up my back and left

shivers in its wake.

Stepping over the threshold, the world didn't suddenly lose all color, turning black and white. The wallpaper didn't peel; the floors didn't creak. The sunshine didn't suddenly get hidden, smothered by the ominous presence of the house.

Instead, the smell of cookies grew stronger, and I noticed the freshly painted walls in a light gray, the sparkling hardwood floors, and the light jazz playing in the background.

Since Mrs. Peabody wore her shoes inside, I kept mine on, as well, following her down a hall to a bright and clean kitchen just as a timer dinged.

"The cookies are ready," she sang. "Have a seat." She slid around the massive island, the polished granite top at odds with the age and style of the house.

I plopped my butt on a stool and remarked, "Your house is gorgeous."

"Thank you. We've been doing some fixes here and there. The joys of owning an older home."

The cookie sheet was placed on top of two pot holders. I almost drooled on them. Utter cookie perfection from their golden color speckled with melted chocolate, to the heavenly aroma wafting up from the pan.

Staring at the treats, I somehow missed Mrs. Peabody pouring a mug of coffee. It landed in front of me, along with a bowl of sugar and a creamer of milk.

Was it wrong that I wanted to marry Mrs. Peabody? The woman oozed sex appeal, and she could take care of a house. Who needed a husband? We'd just invest in dildos.

I sweetened my coffee, as she used a spatula to serve a gooey cookie onto a plate.

"So, Ms. Peterson." The words purred out of her. "What kind of questions do you have that require you to work on such a lovely Saturday?" She leaned on the counter and blinked at me, long lashes over lovely eyes, the red spark in them mesmerizing.

It took an effort to look away. I stared at my coffee, the cream I'd added turning it a light tan color. I took a sip and found it bitter. I added more sugar.

"I visited your husband."

"How is dear Alfred?"

Hanging from the ceiling when he wasn't doing art. "Don't you know?" I asked, looking at her sharply.

She turned away and busied herself at the sink, rinsing dishes and placing them on a rack. "His therapist thought it best that we not disturb him."

"Who's his therapist?"

She waved a hand. "I'm afraid I don't recall his name. Dr. something or other. This whole ordeal has been so mentally exhausting."

The reply seemed off somehow. I mean, we were talking about her spouse. A man she'd been with for more than fifteen years. "Aren't you curious at all about what's happening to your husband?"

"Curious about what? It's quite simple

really. I'm afraid poor Alfred suffered quite a mental break. I blame the stress at his work."

Because helping people find shoes was so hard. Ha.

Given my love of shoes, I could probably make a killing on commission. People would walk into the store, and I'd eyeball their style and feet. I'd whip around, grabbing boxes and flip them at clients like Frisbees. They'd try on the shoes then break into tears because I'd totally understood their arch and sole needs. They'd buy tons of shit, and I'd bring home fat paychecks.

Which made me wonder why I was still a secretary when my obvious dream job was in retail.

However, retail didn't have me investigating dudes who could walk on the ceiling—just like Lionel Ritchie. Was he possessed, too?

"Mrs. Peabody, are you aware that your husband is claiming this house is haunted and that you're possessed?"

Laughter tinkled out of her, bright and clear as bells, yet the hairs on my arm rose. The fact that I had enough hair to rise made me wonder if I should look into waxing or laser hair removal.

"My poor husband. Suffering from such ludicrous delusions. There is nothing wrong with me or the children. Nor this house, for this matter."

"Where are the children?"

"Hanging with their friends, of course." She turned from the sink and wiped her damp hands on a towel before leaning against the counter. "This tragedy has taken such a toll on them, but I felt it best they keep a normal schedule."

"Of course," I muttered.

Mrs. Peabody said all the right things. And yet…ever feel like there was something going on, something you couldn't quite see? In this case, I didn't think it was a case of Meemaw's neighbor sneaking around the apartment building spying on the girls getting undressed at night via the fire escape.

I sipped on my coffee in order to hide my lack of conversation.

Mrs. Peabody smiled widely. So wide that I couldn't help but notice her giant teeth.

All the better to eat me with…

"What do you think of the cookies?"

I'd forgotten about it. Hastily, I brought it to my mouth for a bite. It looked better than it tasted. Dry, flavorless, and possibly less palatable than sawdust. I put it back on the plate and took a gulp of coffee. It didn't mix well with the cookie.

My stomach sloshed unhappily, but I pasted on a smile and said, "Delicious."

"Let me wrap some for you to take when you go."

I couldn't exactly say no, so I let her place some in a bag. I planned to ditch them on the way home. Or maybe I'd arrange to have them delivered to Mike when he didn't make any attempt to contact me.

He won't call. Why would he? He'd been pretty obvious about his dislike of me the first time we met. That moment in his office wouldn't change that.

Maybe I should have saved the smooches and gropes for Sebastian. He'd at least seemed moderately interested in me.

But he never called either.

I realized Mrs. Peabody was looking at me expectantly. Had she spoken while I woolgathered my rejections?

"Excuse me, I missed that."

"I said when will the insurance begin to pay out? While we've covered for the moment the cost of repair, I'm sure my husband's care, even if state mandated, will come at a price."

"I don't make those final decisions. Lots of factors go into it."

"But surely you have an idea." She leaned forward, her features sharper than before, the glint in her eye more red than brown.

An army of ants ran up and down my spine, and my stomach lurched again.

"It's not up to me what happens."

"A shame. Because you are such an interesting girl. A nice-smelling girl." Mrs. Peabody leaned closer and inhaled.

I got the impression she wasn't talking about my perfume. Someone else close to her also showed a keen interest in my scent.

Despite wanting to question her some more, I decided it was time to leave.

"Look at the time," I said as nausea wracked my tummy.

The room wavered, one moment sunny and white. Then, for a moment, dark and dingy, the sink full of dishes, flies dancing in a cloud.

A blink, and everything turned bright again. I, on the other hand, didn't feel so sunny. "I think I should go. I'm suddenly not feeling well."

"Oh, dear." Said with a lack of sympathy and all too much glee. "Would you prefer to lie down? The couch is quite comfortable."

Lie down in this house with her watching over me? The idea didn't appeal.

"No, I'll just go home. Probably just a flu bug." Or something I'd eaten.

"Take these with you. In case you get hungry."

I'd eat dirt before I ate those cookies again.

She thrust the bag she'd filled at me, and I grabbed it, not in the mood to argue or let her know how shitty her cookies tasted. I just wanted out.

As I got to my feet, my vision wavered. I blinked and walked out of the kitchen. The hallway seemed to stretch forever, and sweat beaded on my skin.

Why did I feel so crappy?

How far was that damned door?

I put one foot in front of the other. Focused ahead.

The space tilted, the bright fresh paint fading to a dingy gray. I put my hand out and caught myself on the wall, the edge of a picture frame digging into my palm.

Pictures? I'd not noticed any on my way in. For a moment, I saw a blank gray wall, and then I blinked and saw a family picture taken in the Grand Canyon. Mr. Peabody, his arm around a woman and two gap-toothed children.

Pushing off the wall, I stumbled to the front door, wrenching it open, feeling the warm sun hit my face. I entered the fresh air outside, gladly.

"Bye-bye," cooed Mrs. Peabody. "Hope you feel better soon."

And was it me, or did she add in a muttered, "not," under her breath?

Tottering steps showed the world worked against me, the ground weaving and bobbing as if the whole front yard was at sea. But I'd walked home in a drunken stupor before. I could handle whatever plagued me.

I remained upright, if only barely, reaching the sidewalk without falling over.

Goals!

My truck at the curb looked massive, the lift kit I'd had installed raising it high above the ground. I hoped I could climb into it.

Footsteps behind me showed I had company, and I almost looked over my shoulder.

Almost, but didn't. If this were a horror movie, I'd look back and see that Mrs. Peabody had turned into some grotesque ghoul, fingers stretched for me, her mouth opened wide to eat me.

I reached my truck and yanked open the door, tossing in my stuff as I eyed the height of the driver seat. It felt like climbing Mount Everest getting in. But I made it and slammed the door shut. Locked it, too, before looking out the passenger-side window. The front door of the house was closed. The walkway empty.

And I didn't feel good at all.

Certainly not good enough to drive myself home.

What did that woman do to me?

Good thing I had a plan in case of emergency.

Chloe answered on the second ring, and I croaked, "I've been poisoned. Find my phone."

Why waste time trying to remember an address when she could just use an app? I slumped against the steering wheel, the phone slipping from my grip, her voice hollering my name.

No matter what, Chloe would find me.

Or, at the very least, call in the cavalry. I just wish I hadn't barfed all over him when Dale opened the door to my truck.

Chapter Eight

I felt much better after spewing my guts.

Dale? Not as impressed. Nothing says "nice to see you" like barfing all over a man.

And it didn't look or smell pretty. But good news, it didn't have any blood or body parts in it. Bad news, his shirt soaked it up like a sponge.

I grabbed a bottle of water that I kept in the console cup holder, took a swig to wash out my mouth, then handed it to him.

As he poured it over his face to clear the spatter, I scrounged for some tissue.

During this all, he didn't say a word, and I was struck dumb when he stripped off his shirt and threw it onto the curb.

"Litterbug," I muttered.

The look he gave me stalled anything else I might have said.

"Move over," he growled, hand on the rim of the driver side door. "I'm driving."

Still feeling queasy, I decided it best not to argue.

Dale swung himself into the driver seat, wearing only jeans and his shoes. I rather liked the look, even if he also wore a scowl.

"Are you cold? Would you like my

cardigan?" I offered it and got an evil side-eye, not to be confused with an evil, possessed side-eye that involved a full head rotation.

"Keep the sweater." He started my truck, the big engine growling happily—the slut. Wouldn't you know my truck, like its owner, enjoyed a man's hands on her.

"Who's truck is this?" he asked, pulling away from the curb.

"Mine." Said with great pride.

I got a grunt in reply. Probably one of jealousy because men coveted my vehicle. It brought out something primitive inside. And when the cops pulled me over for supposed road rage, I knew how to flash some cleavage and smile to get out of a ticket.

Dale drove, not speaking to me, and it rubbed me raw.

"Are you going to mope all day because I barfed on you?" I certainly wouldn't have if the roles had been reversed. I'd have offered to hold his hair. What a jerk. He never once offered to hold mine.

I glared at him.

Despite the obvious heat of my stare, he didn't look at me as his hands tightened on the wheel. "I am not moping."

"Then why do you look like your panties are in a twist?"

"Who says I wear any?"

The surprising reply brought a laugh to my lips. "I'll be damned, Scooby, I didn't take you for a man who goes commando. Have you ever had a zipper incident?"

"A man only has one of those in his life before he learns to be careful."

I nodded. "During my natural phase"— where I grew out a bush to rival those of the seventies—"I learned real quick to wear underwear if I planned to throw on some jeans. Waxing is a lot less painful."

"Don't you have any boundaries?" he asked.

I didn't even hesitate. "Nope. And to prove it, I am more than happy to tell you that I now get a Brazilian on a regular schedule."

"Nothing wrong with a bit of bush."

"Says the guy who turns hairy on the full moon."

"The moon doesn't have to be full for us to do it. Those with control can change anytime."

"Do you ever change during sex?"

"No."

"Why not?"

"Because there're laws against bestiality."

"You're still a man inside."

"The answer is still no."

"I think it's cool you can become a wolfman anytime. Show me." I eyed him with curiosity, the conversation distracting from my sore tummy.

"Not now. I'm driving."

"Afraid you might get all slobbery excited over the traffic and chase cars. Gotcha," I said, nodding my head then wishing I hadn't.

"I chase skirts, not cars."

He didn't chase mine, though. Still, he'd come to my rescue. That had to count for something.

"How come you were able to come to me so quick?" I asked. Because he'd literally arrived like two minutes after my phone call. Unless I'd blacked out for longer than I thought.

"I happened to be in the area."

"Why?"

"None of your business."

"Booty call. Probably with a married lady since you won't tell me." Shame. Despite my tryst with Mike, I still had a thing for Dale.

"No, I was not seeing anyone, married or not. Let's leave it at I was looking into something. A better question is, what were you doing there?"

"In case you're wondering, it wasn't a booty call either. I was working on a case, and apparently, the person I was talking to didn't like my questions. I'm pretty sure she poisoned me." My stomach still roiled.

"Poison?" That earned me a skeptical gaze. "That would be pretty brazen considering you were parked out front."

"Then maybe the milk she gave me for my coffee went bad. Something I ate didn't agree with me." My hand rested over my rumbly tummy. "I don't usually puke unless I've had too many hot dogs and go on a whirly ride or try to do a reverse Jersey Turnpike after a few too many drinks."

"I feel so lucky then."

The sarcasm was strong with him. It was strong in me, too. "You're welcome."

He almost smiled. I saw it.

"What were you discussing with Mrs. Peabody?" he asked.

I tossed Dale a suspicious look through one squinted eye. "How do you know her name?" Because I'd certainly not mentioned it. Clarity hit a moment later, and I groaned. "Let me guess. Mike told you."

"Wrong. Your friend Chloe told Pete about Mr. Peabody—"

"And Pete set his most trusted wolves on the case." I jabbed a finger in his direction, two fingers for the two versions of him driving. "But you can stop right now. I am going to solve this mystery."

"No, you're not. Because, as of now, you're off the case."

"Says who?"

"Says me."

"You're not the boss of me." Childish taunts were still the best, especially when your guts were roiling. If he kept trying to piss me off, he might just get soaked again.

"In this, I am your boss, and I say you're done. You're out of your element, kitten. We are dealing with dangerous things here."

"So what? I'm not afraid." Much. One thing was for sure, I definitely didn't suffer from boredom anymore.

"Don't be stupid. I heard about what happened at the asylum."

What a surprise, Mike had tattled. About which part, though? Then again, what were the chances Grumpy admitted he got to second base with me? Or was it third? I was never good at figuring out sports.

"What did you hear?" I asked, hedging my bets.

"That you almost got killed."

"We don't know for sure that Peabody would have hurt me." Although that seemed rather likely had I continued to wear my clothes. An outfit now ruined beyond all repair. Would I have been destroyed, too, if I'd refused to take it off?

"You went to the asylum and deliberately antagonized him."

"I went there to do my job. Not my fault Peabody went all crazy. I was just trying to get at the truth."

"And in doing so, put yourself in danger. Just like you put yourself at risk going to his house." For some reason, he sounded angry. But why? Why did he care what happened to me? "What were you thinking?" He shouted the words as he pulled up in front of my place. Low-rent, co-op apartment in the so-so part of town.

"I was thinking that I wanted to do something with my life, but as usual, I screwed up." Best-laid plans once again fucked up by a girl who rushed in.

"You're damned right you screwed up."

For some reason, his words set me off. "Fuck off. I don't care who the hell you think you are. I don't need you pointing out my mistakes. You're not my boss or my boyfriend. As a matter of fact, you're nobody, which means I don't have to listen to you at all."

Clutching my purse in one hand, because it held a second set of keys, I poured myself out of the front seat. I hit the pavement hard and had to hold on to the door to keep myself upright. Before I could take a step, Dale was there, an arm around my waist supporting me.

I shoved at him, weakly, as if I'd just gone ten rounds with the flu and lost. "Go away. Leave me alone."

"Why are you so damned stubborn?" he muttered.

"Meemaw says I'm assertive." My lips turned down. "It's why people don't like me." The depressing words didn't sit well, and neither did the pity I was sure he had in his gaze.

Once again, I pushed away from him and made it one step, one wavering move where the building doubled, and I wondered how I'd make it all the way to my place.

I'd make it with sheer determination. I dragged another foot forward. The world worked against me and took that moment to tilt.

Before I could kiss the pavement, Dale swept me into his arms.

"Put me down." Protested the girl who was quite content being held.

"Shut up."

"Not possible. I never stop talking."

"I've noticed." He strode right into my building and eschewed the elevator for the stairs.

Show off.

He stopped at the sixth floor and strode

down the hall, stopping exactly in front of my door.

"How come you know where I live?" I asked as he held me securely with one arm, his knee propped under my ass as he jangled my keys to open the door.

"I know a lot of things about you, kitten."

He made it sound so ominous.

The door opened, and he went inside, then kicked it shut before he set me down.

I leaned against the wall, my purse feeling heavy, way too weighty. Peeking out of it was that wretched bag of cookies. Like I'd eat any more of those.

I tossed them on the table by the entrance. I'd burn the fuckers later. Or put them out on my window ledge for those pigeons that liked to roost there and poop.

People might not know, but pigeon poop stank, which meant I kept my windows closed a lot and often thought about buying a BB gun.

Dale kept a hand on my elbow as I tottered to my bathroom. With the vile taste of barf coating my mouth, I was in dire need of a toothbrush.

First, I threw up again. Something about seeing my white porcelain toilet sent me to my knees, heaving up my guts.

But I felt immensely better after, especially once I scrubbed, spat, scrubbed again, gargled, and even flossed until my mouth tasted minty fresh.

Then I went straight to bed. Fuck Dale. My body screamed for sleep.

I passed out almost immediately and

suffered through some truly messed-up dreams, one involving a giant cookie with teeth and red eyes chasing me.

When I woke, a gritty-eyed peek at my clock showed three hours had passed. I staggered into the bathroom, happy that my stomach didn't appear to want to vacate my body anymore. I brushed my teeth and splashed my face, feeling eminently more human. I slipped out of my pretty blue dress for something more comfortable and bra-less. A T-shirt with a piñata that said *I'd hit that* and my track pants that said *Sweet* on the ass.

I exited my bathroom to find Dale still in my apartment.

Great.

With the luck I'd had today, he was probably waiting to start round two of his lecturing. Whatever. Didn't mean I'd listen to it.

I made a beeline for my couch and flopped on it face-first.

"Are you all right? I didn't hear you throwing up again."

He'd heard me puking before? Lovely. Nothing screamed "aren't I sexy?" like blowing chunks. Then again, I'd probably dropped out of any sexy category when I barfed on him at the Peabodys'.

"I'm fine." I waved a hand. "You can go now." I couldn't believe he'd stayed while I slept.

"I don't think so. You seemed pretty sick."

"So sick you didn't call an ambulance?"

"I would have had you shown signs of distress."

"Well, as you can see, no distress. So, you can go now." Leave so I could bang my head on a wall for permanently ruining any chance with Dale.

"I'll go but only if you promise to stop investigating the Peabodys."

"No."

"It's dangerous."

"You're not the boss of me." Chloe was. And even then, I didn't know if I'd listen. Even with my guts feeling as if someone had taken a knife to them, I couldn't quell my curiosity.

Why would Mrs. Peabody try and poison me? Or had her plan merely been to incapacitate me? Had Dale not come along, would I have awoken in her house, tethered to a bed?

Naked…

Who knew what that woman wanted from me.

"Don't make me tie you up again."

At the threat, I turned my head sideways and managed a lopsided smirk. "Have you ever heard that Rihanna song, the one about bondage being exciting?" I propped up my ass on the couch and purred. "Go ahead and spank me."

I expected more grouchy warnings, maybe even a good smack—after all, we had precedence.

Instead, he pulled me off that couch and dragged me to my feet. His hands gripped my wrists tightly. So firmly.

He held me against him and glared down at me.

I smiled.

A low rumble vibrated from him. "You

have got to be the most—"

"Sexy and vibrant woman you've ever met." I helped him finish his sentence. I was helpful like that.

"I was going to say irritating, stubborn, and lacking in common sense sexy woman I've ever met."

"You think I'm sexy?" Focusing on the one word meant my grin widened.

"That's the part you chose to listen to?"

I shrugged. "You say the other things like they're an insult, but my meemaw taught me to embrace my faults. They are part of what makes me, me."

"You are driving me nuts."

"Then leave. Out of sight, out of mind."

"Leaving won't mean out of mind, though. You think I haven't tried to forget you?"

Hold on a second. What? "You've been thinking of me?"

Dale reeled me in closer, and his head lowered so that our noses almost touched. "Every fucking day. Even when I sleep, I see you. You're like some weird addiction I can't shake."

"Why, Dale, that was almost romantic."

"I don't want to be romantic. I want you."

Swoon. The words any girl wanted to hear. But I just had to put my foot in it.

"I feel like I should probably mention that I kissed Mike today."

"What?" He might have yelled the word.

"It happened after the Peabody incident. We ended up in his office, my mouth ended up on his, and next thing you know, he might have touched my va-jay-jay."

"Touched your what?"

I arched a brow. "You know, my girly bits." I hastened to add, "I don't know if it will lead to anything, or even if it means anything. I'm still not entirely sure Mike even likes me, but given he's like your best bud, I feel like I should tell you."

His expression turned stormy. "Did you like it?"

No point in lying at this point. I nodded my head and added, "It was nice." Nice in an explosive, my-body-would-have-enjoyed-seconds kind of way.

"Fuck nice. How does this feel?"

Dale then proceeded to kiss me.

He. Kissed. Me.

And what a kiss. He claimed my mouth. Dominated every inch, cell, and atom of it. Branded me with his embrace. Ignited my passion.

Was it any wonder we ended up on the couch? His heavy body atop mine, my legs parted to cradle him. His hips moved, grinding against me, pushing against my crotch in a way that had me panting and clawing at his bare back.

It was wonderful. And exciting. I wanted more.

When his hand reached under my shirt to cradle my breast, I moaned and arched into his grip. When he pulled back enough to nip at the tip through the fabric covering it, I gasped.

My legs wrapped around his waist, hugging him close as he sucked and nipped at my sensitive nipples. Playing with them. Exciting me so much that a mini orgasm rocked me.

And he knew it.

"That's it, kitten. Wait until I sink my cock into you. I can't wait to feel you clenching it. I want to make you come all over me."

"Yes. Yes. Do it." The dirty talk had me panting and groaning and…meowing?

Dale pulled away, and through heavy eyelids, I got a glimpse of his face, softer than I'd seen it before and yet, at the same time, fierce with passion.

And creased with annoyance.

"Fucking cockblocker." Pulling away from me, Dale yanked a phone from his back pocket and answered it with a barked—human, not wolf—"What now?"

His face lost the sensual connection we'd shared, becoming stonier and harder with each word he heard.

"Yeah. Yeah. I'm coming." And not in a creamy way, I'd wager. "Bye." He shoved the phone away and stared at me.

"I get the impression we're not going to keep making out." Bummer. Two men and two orgasms in one day and yet not a single dick to truly put out the fire in my vagina.

For a moment, he looked pained as he ran his hand through his hair. "Sorry, kitten. I can't stay. That was Mike on the phone." His lips twisted. "I'm needed elsewhere."

Yeah, in my pants, right now. But the mention of Mike kind of threw a bucket of icy water on my ardor. What was I thinking, making out with Mike's best friend? What was Dale thinking, making a pass in the first place? "You should go."

Rising from the couch, he grimaced down at his bare torso. "I don't suppose you have a shirt I could borrow."

I did. Not one he liked, but he put it on anyway.

At the door, he paused, and I thought for a moment he'd say fuck it and take me against the wall. Instead, he said, "Lock the door once I leave. And whatever you do, stay away from the Peabodys."

I crossed my fingers behind my back. "I'll be good." When Hell freezes over.

"Speaking of good..." He stepped into the hall before turning around and giving me a panty-dropping smile. "How would you rate our make-out session?"

I couldn't help myself. I was bad. So bad. Which was why I said, "It was nice," before slamming the door shut.

Dale Interlude

Nice?

She thought that kiss was nice?

Nice was for thoughtful gestures, like a card or flowers on special occasions. Nice was holding open the door for someone going into a building.

Nice shouldn't describe the electric kiss they'd shared.

Argh.

Dale stomped down the stairs and emerged on the sidewalk, his gaze immediately drawn by the truck belonging to Brenda.

Talk about a surprise. When he'd arrived at the Peabodys' place—dropped off by Sebastian on his way to work because of a phone call from Pete telling him to get his ass over there—he'd done a double take.

Who expected a kitten-sized woman to drive a monster truck?

Big all over, even the wheels, and painted a bright electric blue emblazoned with flames along the side, her Dodge diesel-guzzling truck with twenty-two-inch chrome wheels didn't just rumble when you started its three-hundred-and-fifty-nine-cubic-inch engine. It fucking *growled*.

Growled loud enough to give any man

worth his salt a boner. It was a man's truck.

Cute little blondes were supposed to drive Smart cars or practical hybrids, and yet…the fucking thing suited her.

A gray sedan, four-door and practical, which, of course, belonged to Mike, was parked behind the truck.

His buddy got out and whistled. "Damn. That's a fine set of wheels."

"Drives like a dream, too."

"How would you know?" Mike asked, turning to face him.

"Because it belongs to Brenda." Just like Brenda should belong to him.

Not Mike.

Mike, who'd kissed her first, even though he didn't like her.

Mike, who'd touched her first, trying to steal her from Dale.

Crack. Dale's fist hit his friend in the face before he even knew he'd thrown the punch.

Reeling back, Mike rubbed his jaw. His glare almost burnt Dale to a crisp. "What the fuck was that for?"

"Making out with Brenda. I thought we all agreed"—not exactly willingly—"that the girl was off-limits."

"We didn't agree. Pete said Brenda was off-limits on account he's shagging the best friend."

"And you thought what? Fuck Pete? Fuck our promise?" Dale yelled.

"Don't shout at me. The kiss wasn't my fault. She was the one who threw herself on me."

"And did you shove her off?" Dale arched a brow.

A ruddy color filled Mike's cheeks. "Not exactly."

"Not only did you not shove her off, you also fingered her."

"How did you…" Mike's words trailed off as he found his balls and scowled. "It's none of your fucking business what we did."

"I'm making it my fucking business."

"How did you find out?"

"She told me."

Mike bristled. "Which begs the question, what the fuck were you doing with her?"

"Pete asked me for a favor. Seems Brenda decided to go off and do something dangerous on her own. I had to rescue her."

"That woman is a menace to society."

"That woman needs a keeper," Dale said with a snort. *A keeper like me.* "I found her outside the Peabodys' place."

"Peabodys'?" Mike's voice pitched. "Is she fucking stupid? After what happened with the husband this morning?"

"The woman has no sense of self-preservation." Dale shrugged. "Even though she was poisoned by Peabody's wife, she won't back off."

"How do you know she was poisoned?"

"She puked on me."

At that, Mike smirked. "I guess that explains the T-shirt."

Dale didn't have to look down to know

what it said. *Save a Lollipop. Eat a Dick.* A sentiment he couldn't disagree with. At least he'd managed to wash and dry his pants while she napped. As to the underwear he might have handled while doing laundry...he'd succeeded in not sniffing it.

"Let's focus less on my clothing and more on the fact that Peabody's wife felt a need to poison Brenda."

"The same wife nobody's talked to since the day after the fire?" Mike arched a brow.

"The same."

"I thought the house was empty."

Dale shrugged. "So did I." Random knocks and patrols hadn't yielded any signs of life.

"If she's been home this entire time, then why would she answer for Brenda and not us?"

"Fuck if I know, but given the wife tried to poison her and what happened with Peabody, I'm thinking maybe I should keep an eye on her."

At that suggestion, Mike stiffened. "Maybe I should be the one to do that."

"Because she made out with you?"

A smug look crossed Mike's face. "Not my fault she found me irresistible."

"So compelling she called your make-out session 'nice.'"

"Nice?" Mike frowned. "Maybe you misunderstood."

"Nope." Dale hooked his thumbs in the belt loops of his jeans and rocked back on his heels. "She most definitely said your moment together was nice."

A familiar scowl took the grin's place. "I'll

show her nice. What's her apartment number?"

"None of your business. I said I'd handle her."

"Why would…" Mike's eyes widened. "Holy shit, you still have a thing for her."

"So what if I do?"

"The what part is the fact that you just gave me shit for not staying away and keeping my hands to myself."

"That was before. Things have changed."

"Damned right they have. She kissed me." Mike jabbed his chest. "Which means she chose me, so I should get to guard her."

"Don't feel so special, bro. She kissed me, too." A kiss he'd started, but she certainly didn't stop it.

"Was this kiss before or after you found out about the one we shared?"

"After."

"Why, you dirty bastard, you couldn't stand that she chose me."

No, he couldn't. The jealousy was strong in Dale. And for the first time in his life, he'd not followed the bro code, the one that said, "don't touch."

Because he couldn't resist.

Couldn't resist *her*.

"She's mine," Mike snarled.

"Are you sure about that?" Dale retorted.

"I'll show you sure."

Mike lost his cool and dove on Dale. The pair of them exchanging punches, hard smacks as they fought to deal with the first true test of their friendship.

A relationship strained by a woman.

But this woman was special.

So special Dale didn't want to lose, and neither did Mike, apparently, so they brawled in the street until a certain familiar voice hollered from a window. "Scratch the paint on my truck, and I will rip off your balls and feed them to the lions at the zoo."

The window slammed shut, hiding Brenda from sight, but it did its job. The fizzle had left the fight.

Dale stared at a glowering Mike. "Truce?"

Mike eyed the hand Dale held out. "I'm not giving up."

"Neither am I. But I also don't want to fight you."

A sigh heaved out of Mike. "Me either. But where do we go from here?"

Where indeed.

I want her. Mike wants her.

"I guess we're both going to chase her until she chooses one." Dale smiled. "May the best wolf"—*me!*—"win."

Chapter Nine

Whatever crap Mrs. Peabody put in her coffee and cookies had hit me hard. I may have stopped puking—thank goodness because that would have put a damper on my interrupted make-out session with Dale—but I still felt weak.

I also felt guilty. It didn't take a genius to realize that Mike and Dale fought over me in the street. Which meant, along with the guilt, I experienced a good dose of elation.

Hello, two guys fighting over a girl? Super sexy. But sad, too. I guess it meant they weren't into sharing, which would have really been the ideal scenario.

Who would have thought three close buds, in this day and age where reverse harems were the norm, would be so old school?

Could I be content settling for one man? A funny question given, just a day ago, I had *no* man in my life. Now, I appeared to have two vying for my affections. Could they come to an agreement and share?

It had happened to Chloe. When Pete and Anthony first got involved with her, they hated each other. Out of love for Chloe, they'd learned to get along, and now they seemed to share her without a problem.

However, that didn't mean Mike and Dale would do the same.

If that were the case, if I could have only one, how would I choose?

With my mind muddled, I chose to not make a decision. Fatigued by my ordeal and dilemma, I went back to bed.

And dreamed. Oh boy, did I dream.

Dreamed I sprinted like a crazy woman, which totally wasn't my thing. Short legs were made for walking, cute skirts, and footstools to reach high places. Yet, here I was, panting, my lungs burning with physical exertion because I ran as if my life depended on it.

My boobs, a respectable C cup, jiggled with each jolting step, and branches whipped my naked skin much like a riding crop would.

Which begged the question, why was I buck naked in the woods?

Stopping, I planted my hands on my hips and looked down. It was me all right, from my Brazilian waxed mound to my tits, the left one slightly larger than the right and the nipples fatter than I liked. All me, in the buff, in the dark, outside.

While not averse to skinny-dipping, there wasn't a lake around. Rather, I appeared to be on the edge of a park.

Ahead of me, a swing set, the wide metal legs spaced in a triangle, sat silent, the chains holding the seats still. The monkey bars painted in a bright array of primary colors were empty, as were the benches the mommies and their strollers liked to park at. Good thing they were vacant. If anyone saw me, they'd probably call the cops.

Then again, I doubted too many people would be out this time of night with their little demonic darlings. Shouldn't children be in bed at this hour? I could be wrong, though. After all, how many times had I gone to a fine restaurant later in the evening and listened to a child testing the limits of their lungs while the clueless parents sat on their phones ignoring them?

Personally, I would have left the baby home with a nanny. Nothing should ever interfere with a good meal.

But I wasn't in a restaurant, I was in a park, all alone, not a single soul around. Probably not a good idea, especially since I had no clue how I'd gotten there.

"Don't tell me those cookies had LSD in them." The last time I'd sleepwalked was after an incident with some special brownies. I'd woken up in the fridge, splayed in piles of food and definitely not as sexy as that movie *Nine and a Half Weeks* made it look. It probably explained why the guy I ate the brownies with never called back.

Creak. Creak. The swing seats began to move, swaying back and forth on their chains, not a breath of air or a pair of hands to push them.

Fucking freaky. I didn't pee down my leg, not yet.

Just because something screwed with me wasn't a reason to be afraid. Add to that the fact I'd waited all my life—and watched countless horror flicks—kind of hoping for my own supernatural moment.

Finally. It was happening.

Don't fuck it up.

I waved. "Hello, Mr. or Mrs. Ghostie."

Not even a moan replied, but the swings stopped dead. The silence somehow grew heavier, pressing on me, and the darkness thickened despite the park lights.

The skin at my neck prickled, and I couldn't help but whip my head around. There was nothing there, nothing I could see, yet the sensation of being watched increased.

I fully turned and squinted into the darkness, but the trees on the edge of the park didn't reveal anything, not even a pervert whacking off at the view of my perfect and naked body.

Turning back, I squeaked, like a mouse caught in a trap, because standing behind the swings, tall, taller than a human, hairier than one, too, was a wolfman with glowing golden eyes.

The hair on his body appeared dark, thick, and lush. His shoulders were broad, his legs oddly jointed, and his face pulled into a muzzle. As for farther down his body, below his waist, he definitely showed signs of liking what he saw.

I, on the other hand, wasn't into fornicating with the wildlife, so I took a step back and winced as my bare foot left the soft sand of the play area for the coarser gravel of a path.

The pain I could tolerate, and a pedicure would fix any damage; however, I still froze at the warm puff of air against my hair, followed by an audible sniff.

Oh, shit. Something is behind me.

Although it went against my self-preservation instincts, I still whirled around and squealed like a pig with its tail yanked when I saw a second wolfman standing right behind me, close enough that I could reach out and touch.

I didn't want to touch. I didn't want to be here, alone and naked, with two wolfmen. My sense of adventure only went so far.

The horror movies advised against making sudden moves. I knew better than to show fear in front of a predator, but my humanity—and perhaps a bit of proper girly fear—kicked in, and I took off running.

No surprise, like any prey that bolted, I gave them the perfect excuse to chase.

For the second time that night, I found myself running and very unimpressed by it all.

Why was this happening? Since when did wolfmen play in my park? Shouldn't they have a leash? Did they not see the signs?

I bolted across the lawn, the dew of the grass sticking to my feet, knees pumping to my chest, yet knowing there was no way I could escape. How could I outrun two large predators?

My bladder clenched tightly when something howled behind me. Those Kegel exercises I'd done had just proven their worth. I didn't let loose a stream down my leg, but I did loose a litany of curses to make even Meemaw blush.

"Goddamn, motherfucking, leg-humping

bastards, where's my gun when I need it?" Certainly not on me, unless I'd tucked it in my va-jay-jay before embarking on my nocturnal stroll.

I'd almost reached the sidewalk, which really didn't offer any extra protection, when something hit me from behind. Like a tree, I went timber as I hit the grass.

I scrambled to my knees, fingers clawing at dirt, survival instinct kicking in, determined to keep fighting, not willing to die.

A hairy body covered mine, the fur coarse and thick, tickling against my skin. The hot breath of the beast puffed against the skin of my back. A freakishly long arm wrapped around my middle, the paw end of it tipped in claws, but they didn't dig into my skin.

The wolfman did, however, yank my ass backwards, hard against him, hard enough I felt a need to exclaim, "Get that thing away from my va-jay-jay."

To my relief, the beast didn't take advantage of me, and it took a moment for me to realize I no longer felt fur against me or claws but flesh and hands. Powerful hands that manhandled me onto my back and then gripped my wrists to pull them above my head. My captor stretched my body and pinned it under a very masculine and aroused one.

Familiar brown eyes stared down at me.

"Dale!" I might have screeched his name. "What is wrong with you trying to scare me like that?"

"You're not scared." His straight white teeth with pronounced canines appeared in a wide smile.

"Really? Then explain why my heart is racing."

"Exertion is part of it, but do you know what else I smell…" He nudged me, a gentle rub of his nose on mine as he whispered, "Excitement."

Yes, this was exciting, and also possibly dangerous. If a cop drove by and saw us naked on the ground, he'd assume the worst. He'd probably arrest us for indecent acts in public.

I'd have a criminal record.

Awesome. I'd be a badass. A rebel. Meemaw would freak. I'd have to get a tattoo.

"I'm almost afraid to ask why you're smiling," Dale said.

"Can't a girl be happy for no reason?" I wiggled my hips. "So, what's a nice wolf like you doing in a place like this?"

"You tell me. It's your dream."

"Dream?" This wasn't real? Bummer. But at the same time, the possibilities…

"Why did you call me into your dream, kitten? Did you need me to finish something?" He punctuated his query with a thrust of his hips.

Heat pooled in my sex at the feel of his cock nudging at my clamped thighs. My nipples tightened as the skin on his chest brushed them.

Did I want to finish what we'd started? Kiss that delectable mouth again? Let him take me, his hard cock thrusting, his body heavy on top of mine?

Yes!

What about Mike? He'd kissed and touched me, too, and I liked it just as much. Didn't he also deserve a chance?

Before I could even answer myself, the lovely naked body atop mine got torn off, and I could hear some cursing and thumping of fists meeting flesh.

Sitting up, I gaped. It appeared, by merely thinking of Mike, I'd called him. Or had he always been there, the second wolfman in my dream, silent until now?

Whatever the case, I had two naked men in my fantasy, and neither of them was playing with me. Talk about my subconscious working against me.

Forking two fingers in my mouth, I whistled, loud and shrill. The strident notes stopped them dead.

I waved and smiled. "Oh, fellas. I'm over here. No need to fight when you can share."

"Share?" Dale spat the word out as he tossed his head, flinging hair out of his face.

Mike made an equally disgusted face. "What makes you think I want sloppy seconds?"

I frowned. "Ain't nothing sloppy about this body, mister. I am tight." A coy smile. "Why don't you come see for yourself?"

Nothing like the promise of sex to wipe the light of battle from a man's face. The guys untangled themselves and stood to face me.

Ack. Someone fetch me a fan or some smart pills because I was struck dumb, and speechless. I was also erotically punched in the va-jay-jay because…wowzers!

Standing in the flesh—if dream flesh counted—were two epic examples of manhood.

Chiseled abs, the kind made for licking, tapered waists with sexy V's I wanted to trace, muscled thighs, perfect for bouncing me on, and thick arms, meant to hold me up as they pounded me while standing.

But the *pièce de résistance*: epic-sized cocks.

As they stared at me, Dale sizzling with heat and promised danger, Mike with a hint of anger and fierce passion, I couldn't help but feel a quiver in my sex. A hunger in my loins. A need for not one of these men but both, dammit! Call me greedy, but I felt fairly confident I could handle it. And if I couldn't? I'd die orgasming.

I leaned back on my elbows and wantonly parted my thighs. *Don't judge.* This was my wet dream, and I could do whatever I wanted, and I wanted to do them both.

"Anyone want a taste of honey?"

"I thought I smelled something sweet," Dale growled.

So sexy. It made my insides quiver. Lying flat on the ground, no longer caring where I was but wishing I'd chosen a bed instead of grass, I kept my gaze on the guys as I ran my hands down my body. They watched and liked, so evident in the way their cocks rose and lengthened.

Oh, my.

Licking my lips, I managed a husky, "Are you both just going to look at me all night?"

"What do you want?" asked Dale. He

sauntered toward me, hips rolling, cock jutting proudly, a beast on the prowl.

"You know what I want. Your tongue tasting me. Your cock fucking me." Not shy in real life, I didn't hold back in my dream.

"What about me?" snapped Mike.

My gaze moved to him, the gruff mask hinting at vulnerability. I recognized it because I suffered from it, and like him, I hid it.

"I want you both."

"We don't share." This from Dale.

"But what if I can't choose?"

"Surely, there's one you like better," said Mike.

"Maybe if you both gave me a sample, I could decide." I batted my lashes, and yet I could see them holding back.

Hell no.

I licked a finger and let it trace its way down, down until I found my sweet spot.

The men stood frozen, and hard. So very, very hard.

"It's a dream, lighten up," I whispered.

Magic words, or finally all the blood left their brains, and they stopped overthinking it because one moment I lay along on the ground alone and, the next, I had a body pressed to my front, and since they'd rolled me on my side, I had a body pressed against my back.

Sweet heat and arousal rushed through me as two sets of hands began to roam my flesh. Two distinct mouths traced paths on my skin.

"That's better," I murmured. "See, isn't it

nicer when we all play together?"

"You talk too much," growled Dale. His lips claimed mine, scorching with passion, the press of them fierce, so fierce I moaned.

Or did I moan because Mike sucked that sensitive spot on my nape? Did it matter? It felt amazing.

Decadent.

Right.

And to think they were arguing against it. Could there be anything better than being smooshed between their bodies, their evident maleness pressing against me?

I panted in between kisses, squirming against their bodies, the skin-to-skin touch electric. I pushed my ass against the hard erection behind me. From the front, Dale's fingers dug into my hip as he thrust and ground against me, his cock trapped between our bodies, and still, the friction of his hard length against my lower belly proved exciting.

As if they suddenly both had the same brilliant idea, I found myself flat on my back as a pair of mouths each latched onto a nipple.

Holy hell. I squirmed and writhed and panted as their hot tongues, surely double jointed and devilishly long, swirled around my nipples. Their lips tugged the turgid flesh, pulling it before sucking it, alternating their movements so that I was in a constant state of extreme arousal.

When they bit into my skin, I cried out and grabbed their heads, my fingers sifting through hair different in length and texture, another reminder that a pair of them pleasured me.

A part of me struggled to remember this was a dream when it felt so real and so right.

Who cares if I'm only imagining this? The pleasure was real. And I wanted more.

I wanted them to take turns fucking me. To fill me up with cocks, to thrust into me, bringing me to the edge of ecstasy and then tossing me over.

Instead, I got their fingers, one from each man, penetrating me, finger fucking me, driving me closer and closer to the edge. My hips arched off the ground, and they pushed me back down.

Held me down as one tugged at my nipples and the other man, oh God, the other one nuzzled my cleft.

His hot tongue—

A car horn, strident and insistent, woke me suddenly. Sweaty, aroused, and most definitely alone in my bed.

"Fuck me," I muttered. Couldn't the rude person outside have waited a minute longer? I was so close. My poor flesh ached, yearning for the climax it had almost achieved.

Squirming on the sheets, I realized I needed satisfaction. Perhaps Dale and Mike weren't here, but that didn't mean I couldn't take care of myself.

I kicked off the sheets and shimmied out of my underwear, my T-shirt not long enough to get in my way.

Lying on my back, I drew up my knees and let my thighs part, exposing myself to touch.

My finger found my moist slit and

penetrated, dipping into my honeypot, finding it already soaking wet.

Drawing my finger out, I used my wet digit to rub my clit, pleasuring myself with nimble strokes. Imagining more masculine and callused fingers on my flesh, stroking me, a hot tongue licking me.

Shudder.

I did so love to be licked.

My second hand reached down and penetrated my hungry pussy while my other hand continued to stroke my clit. In and out I thrust, imagining a stiff cock and hard body atop me.

I could still remember the feel of the lips, hard against mine. The bodies hot against my skin.

As I worked myself faster and faster, my hips arched off the bed, and I might have howled when I came.

I just couldn't have said who I howled most for.

Mike Interlude

Looking Dale in the eye proved a little difficult the next morning, the erotic dream Mike experienced still weighing on him.

Since when do I fantasize about getting into a threesome with my buddy and a girl?

Since when did he lust about a girl he wasn't even sure he liked?

While his mind might not yet know exactly how he felt about her, his body did. The moment they'd shared had left him unsettled. Wanting.

Hungry…

And he didn't hunger alone.

Usually, knowing Dale or Sebastian also lusted for a chick would make him back off. He wasn't into macho games of posturing or vying for affection. Mike wasn't a guy looking for a permanent entanglement, and yet…something about Brenda drew him. Something about her made him want to throw his usual misgivings to the side.

He wanted her.

But so did Dale.

Only one could have her, though.

Or could they manage to share?

Mike couldn't help but recall the sense of

rightness from his dream, the erotic pleasure of worshipping a woman with his best friend at his side.

Had he suddenly turned bi without knowing it?

Eyeing Dale as he entered the kitchen, Mike didn't find himself engulfed in lust. Didn't want to grab his buddy by the ass.

What did it mean?

I'm the shrink. Shouldn't I know? Could it be that, in this case, he could perhaps find it in him to share?

Then again, it wasn't just up to him. There was Brenda to consider, and then Dale himself.

Could Dale come around to the way of thinking that so many around the world already had, that sharing one woman, without jealousy, was possible?

Interesting tidbit…Mike noted that Dale had a problem meeting his gaze.

Did he also have the dream? Surely not. Dream walking was something for witches and Native Americans, not a modern-day wolf.

Mike must be imagining things. Then again, maybe he wasn't because Sebastian, after a moment of silent eating, asked, "What's up with you two? You're both acting like you had a fight."

"A tiny one. No big deal," Dale replied. "We're all good now."

Were they? Yes, they'd stopped fighting enough to get into a car together and go do some investigating for Pete, but they never actually talked about anything.

There wasn't really any time. All too soon after leaving Brenda's, they found themselves engrossed in a new witch killing across town.

Either the wizards had fucked up destroying the demon, or there was another one on the loose, or so the evidence indicated.

The crime scene had one body, that of a witch, torn apart. Blood missing. Chunks of flesh gone. However, the bite marks were much smaller than in the previous cases. And Pete indicated a few, stating, "I think there was more than one creature here."

More than one, with a smaller dentition, a different bite mark entirely, which made them all wonder, was it a demon or something else?

"What did you fight about? Was Mike making you listen to his jazz channel again?" Sebastian teased, oblivious to the source of tension.

Since he kept enough secrets because of his work with disturbed patients, Mike didn't like keeping any at home. "We ran into Brenda yesterday."

"What?" Sebastian straightened from his slouch. "I thought she was off-limits on account she was Pete's girlfriend's best friend."

"Yes, was, *is*," Mike emphasized, "off-limits. I didn't hunt her down on purpose. I ran into her at work."

"And she kissed him," Dale added.

"She kissed Mike?" Sebastian didn't have to sound so incredulous.

Mike glowered.

"Don't be too worried. She called it *nice*," Dale mocked.

"Don't be so smug," Mike snapped. "She said the same thing about you."

"Hold on a second, you both kissed her?"

"Kissed and groped. But we didn't go all the way if that's what you're asking," Dale replied.

No, they hadn't, though Mike didn't admit that had she not walked away, he would have totally claimed her. On his desk. The very idea of it so wildly out of character, yet he hoped she'd come back to finish what they'd started.

Sebastian slapped his hand on the table. "Totally unfair. I thought we'd made a pact to stay away from her. And now I find out you're both making out with her behind my back."

"Not behind your back since it only happened yesterday and we're telling you now."

"So, who's getting her?"

While the word "me" sat on the tip of his tongue, Mike held back. "No one."

"Let's not be hasty," Dale interjected. "She's obviously interested."

"So you want to let her choose?" Mike wouldn't fare so well in a straight-up competition with Dale. He lacked some of the suave moves and pretty words his friend used so easily.

"Hey, if we're letting her decide, then I should get a turn, too. After all, I was interested before Mike was."

Add Sebastian to the mix with his long hair and flirty manner?

It wasn't just Mike who growled, "Fuck

no."

Dale continued. "Let's not make this more complicated than it has to be."

"In other words, two's company but three's a crowd," Sebastian bitched.

Actually, three was a ménage, but Mike kept his mouth shut. Despite today's laws encouraging women to have harems to keep the male population in check, he wasn't sure how he felt about it.

How would he handle jealousy?

Sharing her body?

I can't. He wanted her to himself.

Still, that dream…that fantasy almost made him think another way was possible.

Madness.

Or the only way to win her over?

One thing's for sure, if I want any kind of chance with her, I'm going to have to be nice. Even if it killed him.

Chapter Ten

Feeling in fine form Sunday morning, I was all smiles and sunshine for my weekly brunch with my BFF.

The mimosas were already ordered, and a plate heaped with bacon to nibble on already sat on the table while I waited for Chloe to arrive.

She entered the café we'd been coming to for years. Spotting me, she came over. Alone.

"What happened to your men?" I asked. These days, it was rare to see her without at least one of them.

"Preparing to make some room for Pete's stuff at Anthony's place."

I almost spewed my drink—which would have been a waste of alcohol. I swallowed quickly and said, "What happened to Pete not wanting to live with 'Fang Boy?'"

"They finally realized that bouncing back and forth was driving me nuts. I mean, I'd go to get dressed for work, only to realize my good skirt was at Anthony's or I'd left my makeup at Pete's."

"You should have kept your place and made them come to you."

A shadow crossed her face. "I couldn't go back. Not after what the demon did."

Stupid me for having forgotten. The cleaners and painters had done a good job eradicating the damage, but the memory still haunted my friend.

"No sad faces. Not today. Today, we celebrate."

"What are we celebrating?" Chloe lifted her glass.

"The fact that Peabody is 100 percent possessed."

"I heard something about an incident at the asylum."

"Incident?" I arched a brow. "Dude was dancing on the ceiling. You should have seen it, Chloe."

She grimaced. "No, thank you. Seeing one demon was enough for me. I'll stick to watching it on the television screen."

"It wasn't that bad."

"Did you or did you not almost die?"

I made a disparaging noise. "Bah, I'm sure Mike would have stopped Peabody before he hurt me." Mike probably didn't know it, but I was sure he harbored a hero inside. If only I'd not suddenly decided to have some morals and walked out on him before we got to test the sturdiness of his desk.

"Speaking of hurting...care to explain what happened yesterday afternoon?" She spoke sternly to me, and I couldn't help but feel chagrinned.

Chloe had tried calling me the night before, but exhausted, I'd fired her a text saying I was all right and I'd see her at brunch.

"I went to Peabody's house."

"After I told you not to?" Chloe tsked as she shook her head.

"I thought I'd be okay. I mean, I'd just seen Mr. Peabody, and it was obvious he was possessed. I honestly thought there wouldn't be any danger."

"Obviously, you were wrong. If I didn't know better, I'd have thought someone slipped you a mickey. What happened to you?"

"Peabody's wife slipped me a mickey."

"She what?"

"Drugged me or poisoned me. I'm not entirely sure, but whatever it was made me barf my guts out." All over poor Dale, who somehow looked past it to still try and get with me.

Imagine that, a guy not scared off by my mouth, attitude, or barf. So why couldn't I just choose him over Mike?

"Are you okay?" Chloe's face creased in concern. "Why didn't anyone tell me? I would have come over."

"And done what, watch me sleep?" I snorted. "Please. I'm a big girl." Still, it was nice that Dale had stuck around for a bit instead of taking off. But even nicer would have been if one of the guys had checked on me that evening or asked to spend the night. After all, someone had poisoned me.

"Have you seen a doctor?"

"No, nor do I plan to."

"Brenda." She stretched my name.

"Why would I waste a visit? Still alive."

"Still blonde," Chloe grumbled. "And

dumb. You should have gone to a hospital to have your stomach pumped."

"I puked enough on my own, thank you very much."

"Stop being a smartass," Chloe snapped. "I'm worried about you."

"I feel fine." I leaned forward to put my hand over hers. "Really, I do."

"You better. Love you," Chloe said, her voice thick.

"Me, too. Admit it, what you're really worried about is Mrs. Peabody having designs on my body."

At that, Chloe snorted. "You think everyone has designs on your body."

True. "More seriously, I think she was planning to do something nefarious"—God I loved that word— "to me, but I escaped the house just in time."

"A good thing Dale was close by to rescue you."

"Thanks for calling in the cavalry."

"Anytime. I have to ask, how did Mrs. Peabody drug you?"

"She lured me with coffee and cookies." I still shuddered at the thought of those cookies.

Getting up this morning, I'd noticed the plastic baggie still on the console table. Only when I grabbed it, there weren't any cookies inside but rather some kind of sludge squirming with maggots.

If there'd been anything left in my stomach, I would have barfed again. In that moment, I made a vow to myself and my ass to never eat any cookies again unless they came out of a box from the store.

You didn't really think I'd abstain from cookies forever, did you?

"But why would she do that?" Chloe's forehead knitted into a frown. "She had to know we'd trace any disappearance back to her."

That was the part where my theory fell apart. "If she was possessed like her husband, would she really care?"

"Speaking of possessed." Chloe leaned forward. "Don't say anything, but there might be another demon on the loose."

"No." I breathed the word, more excited than horrified. Stupid. I know. But talking about demons and possession and attempted kidnapping was much more exciting than the lottery pool at work we had for the PowerBall coming up.

"Pete says it looks like there might be up to three demons this time. Smaller ones. They're working on getting some proper dental molds to be sure. Anthony's also running some trace evidence to see if the genetic markers match the demon genome."

Anthony, being long-lived, had access to things humans could only write about in books or dream up in movies. It was enough to make me insanely jealous.

"Is this possible new demon part of the reason why Pete's moving in?"

Chloe rolled her shoulders. "It's hastening the process, shall we say."

"If they're that worried about you, then why are you here alone?"

"Not alone." She pointed out the window to a car.

Imagine that, I knew the guy sitting in it.

"He's got Dale guarding you?"

My jealousy meter went up like a thousand notches.

"Only for a few hours. Then Pete needs Dale elsewhere."

"With him worrying about your safety, does this mean I'm going to have the wolf pack dictating"—the verbal kind not the cream filled—"to me again?"

"Maybe. Anthony thinks that last time the only reason the demon came after me was because of his involvement in the case. Some kind of rivalry thing between their kinds."

Demons versus Vampires. I think I'd played that once at the arcade.

"So I'm safe?" Bummer. Not that I wanted three guys cramping my style. Although giving me a cramping charley horse because of strenuous activities in bed? Whole other thing.

We spent the rest of breakfast chatting about more mundane things while eating copious amounts of food. Being a nice girl—who still wanted to get in someone's pants—I had the restaurant send out a Styrofoam food container filled with carbs.

Didn't want Dale fainting should he require energy for later.

As for me, my appetite had returned. My

tender tummy needed filling after the rude abuse of the previous day. By the time we stepped out of the restaurant, I was bloated and happy.

Being full meant I felt a need to suck it in at the sight of Dale, standing outside his car, leaning against it, dressed in snug blue jeans and a button-down shirt, the sleeves rolled up to show the muscles of the forearms he held crossed over his chest.

Being a good friend, I walked Chloe over to her ride and smiled. "Hey, Scooby."

"You're looking better, kitten."

"Feeling better, too. Not that you would know." I sniffed, a girly sniff, which required me jabbing an elbow at my best friend, who snickered.

"Actually, I did know. I peeked in on you last night just to be sure."

"You did not."

"I did too. You were sleeping."

I blinked. "How would you know? I had the door chained shut."

"Fire escape." He smiled. "At least you're smart enough to keep the window locked."

Chloe's gaze bounced between us, and I could see her mind working furiously. I only wished the conclusion she came to matched a reality I wanted.

"A lock wouldn't keep a real man out," I sassed. "But it does keep the riffraff and animals away."

"Not really. If an animal wanted you, nothing would stop him."

Was I the only one hearing the innuendo?

"How come you were out and about last night?" Or did he only come to see me?

"There's been another murder."

"I heard. Chloe says we might be looking at three demons."

He shrugged. "Maybe."

"But..." I prodded.

"Something about it seemed different. The bite marks weren't just smaller, they weren't the same as those on the other witch victims we encountered before."

"Could it be a different type of demon?"

"Could be. It's not like we have a guideline when it comes to them."

"How about we not talk about demons?" Chloe hugged herself as she shivered. "If you ask me, I'd be happier finding out a pack of rabid squirrels attacked than another one of those things."

"Whatever it is, it's deadly, which means you shouldn't be out alone," he said, glancing up and down the street.

"I'm not a witch."

"Maybe not, but you did grab the attention of whatever is haunting the Peabodys."

I flapped a hand in nonchalance. "Bah. I'll be fine. How much trouble can I get into at the library?" All those dusty books. Gross. I wasn't keen on the whole reading part, but a girl had to do what a boy told her not to do.

"You, in a library?" His lips pursed. "This better not be about the Peabody case. I told you to stop looking into it."

At that, Chloe snickered. "Like telling her no is going to work. Have you met Brenda?"

"I have. She needs a keeper."

I couldn't help a flirty smile. "Are you volunteering, Scooby?"

A slow smile pulled at his lips. "Maybe I am. Get in. I'll drop you off."

"No, thanks. I've got Big Blue with me." I waved down the street to my truck.

"I know, and I am still telling you to get your ass in that car. I'll drop you off at the library and pick you up when you're done. That way, I know you'll be safe." He reached for me, but I skipped away.

"No, thanks. But if you're that concerned about me, feel free to stop by tonight with a pizza. And beer," I yelled as I skipped away to my truck.

"You are the most annoying woman to deal with," he hollered back.

"I know." Part of my charm. Take it or leave it.

Hopefully, he didn't see my crossed fingers that he'd take a chance on me.

Was it wrong to hope he'd bring his friends?

Dale Interlude

"I want to throttle her," Dale muttered as he slid into the car.

A boisterous belly laugh burst out of Chloe. "Everyone does. That's what makes Brenda so special."

"I'll say she's special, in a needs-a-helmet kind of way. She has no sense of self-preservation."

"No, she doesn't. Brenda embraces every new thing she comes across without thinking of the consequences."

"She's going to get hurt if she doesn't start being more careful."

Chloe's lips pulled down. "I know, which is why she could use a good man or two or three in her life."

"Has she said so? Is she looking to settle down with a harem?" Despite knowing he sounded like a pussy, Dale couldn't help but ask. Someone get the gun and shoot him now.

"Not in so many words, but let's face facts. Brenda's a handful, and while I know all she really wants is one person to love her, being that she's so energetic, I think part of the reason relationships fail for her is because she overwhelms people."

He could see that happening. Brenda was constantly go, go, go. He liked that about her and, at the same time, hated it. How did Chloe handle it? "You've been friends for a long time, right?"

Chloe nodded.

"She doesn't overwhelm you."

"Don't kid yourself. Being with her is like being sucked into a tornado, chaos and noise all the time. But there's a reason why we never shared a room at college or an apartment. I can't do it twenty-four-seven." Chloe hastened to add, "That's not to say I don't love her. Brenda is my best friend. I would step in front of a bullet for her. However, if we ended up in a bomb shelter alone, the last two people on earth..." Chloe shrugged. "I'd probably shoot myself."

"Not her?"

"I told you, she's my best friend. I'd never hurt her. I want what's best for her."

"And you think what's best is a harem of guys because you don't think I could handle her alone."

"Maybe you could. I mean, you'd certainly try." Chloe shrugged. "However, once you moved in, and it's just the two of you, all day, every day, with her bouncing off the walls and talking non-stop..."

"Afraid I'll choke her to death?" He said it with a grin.

"That would be better than breaking her heart. She's had that happen enough in her life."

Someone had hurt Brenda? Give him an address, he'd kick their ass. "What happened to her?"

"It's not my place to talk about it. Let's just say boyfriends aren't the only people in her life who've left her. She deserves better than the shit hand life has dealt her. She deserves love, so if you're not ready to fully commit, then don't lead her on."

Love? Was what he felt for Brenda anything close to that emotion? Lust, he had no trouble recognizing. A certain possessive need, definitely. But love?

Would a man in love contemplate sharing her with his best friend?

Would a man in love call Sebastian and ensure his friend went to the library to keep an eye on her, even knowing that long-haired Casanova would probably make a play?

Would a man in love have dreams of tag teaming her body?

If only he could figure out the answer. He certainly didn't want to hurt Brenda. But Chloe raised some valid points. In, or out. He couldn't hover halfway.

Dale dropped off Chloe at Pete's, who swung her into his arms, grabbed her ass, and planted a kiss.

What a change from a few months ago. Pete, once upon a time, didn't believe in ménage relationships, yet was now fully involved in one with a vampire he'd started out hating.

If Pete can do it, can I?

Dale, at least, didn't hate Mike or Sebastian. But could he handle the jealousy?

Leaving the smooching pair—and feeling an urge to adjust his nut sac to erase the taint of their cutesy display—he headed next to a brownstone in the middle of the city. A nondescript place with a discreet sign advertising physiotherapist services by appointment only. Easing some tension in his muscles wasn't why he entered the building, though.

The fake business served to hide a cryptozoid installation. One of the many secret offices of the TDCM. They had them scattered around the country, the world, each serving a different purpose from administration, incarceration, immigration—because some species couldn't move into some places without causing a minor war. Underneath the layers of human bureaucracy existed another hidden layer, one to serve the non-humans.

This particular installation was dedicated to scientific research. As to his presence, Dale had come in person to hear the autopsy results on the witch.

First, though, he had to sign in.

The receptionist, a silver-haired lass with her pointed ears hidden, fixed him with an emerald gaze. "Remove your weapons and place them in the basket."

The gun in his ankle holster hit the bottom of the white wicker basket along with his pocket knife. Some might find it ironic that a shapeshifter chose to carry physical weapons. Dale, however, knew of the dangers in the world and liked to hedge his bets. Where claws didn't work, an iron blade or silver bullet might.

"Please sign in here." A perfectly manicured nail tapped the raised counter.

"I know." The fact that Dale had been in this office countless times before did not thaw her demeanor or instructions. Each time, with a serious mien, she watched as he placed his palm on the seemingly innocuous stone countertop that ran the length of the reception desk.

A bell chimed. At times, Dale wondered what would happen if it didn't. Would the slight receptionist suddenly stand with a flamethrower and roast him? Or was this like the department of justice for the cryptos that dropped cages onto aggressive complainants seemingly out of nowhere?

"Please proceed through the door to your left." She pointed, even knowing he didn't need direction.

The frosted-paned portal opened with a simple push, and Dale found himself in a smaller room, bereft of furniture, the only décor some silver hooks lined across the wall with some white coats hanging from them.

More decoration than anything else. The next step involved sterilization before he even got close to the labs.

"Assume the position." The melodic tone emerged from no visible speaker, and he had to wonder if the elf maiden even moved her lips at the front desk when she spoke.

Knowing the drill, he stood still and held his arms out from his sides.

The light in the room brightened, and his skin tingled as magic swept over him, touching him in places that should remain private. All of him, inside and out, heated then cooled. His teeth vibrated as an electrical current passed through him.

It took but a moment before the voice declared, "You are clear of enchantments and curses. Please proceed."

What would happen if, just once, he did have some kind of magic miasma clinging to him?

Then again, given how seriously the TDCM took themselves, he probably didn't want to know.

The next door out of the room opened onto a long corridor. A series of closed doors with plaques to identify them marched down the hall.

Having been here before, Dale knew he wanted the last door, the one reserved for autopsies.

In a stroke of luck, Pete and his pack had managed to keep the latest witch death off the human radar. In other words, the cops didn't know, so the TDCM had swept in and taken over the crime scene, removing the body and all evidence of the murder.

Should the humans come looking, they'd find nothing but a clean and abandoned house. Just another person who'd suddenly decided to pull up roots and leave.

It happened all the time. Especially with their kind. Having most of the cryptozoids come out to the general public didn't mean they wanted the humans involved in their business.

The truth the humans knew only scratched the surface of the crypto reality. And it was best to keep it that way. The Salem Witch trials and the Inquisition and other great sweeps against magic remained as reminders of what happened when magic and those considered non-human got too complacent with their lives. Lycans got hunted to the point that their numbers were severely culled for years. The mermaids found themselves struggling as fishermen took over the seas. And the Sasquatch kept running from the damned paparazzi.

Dale knocked lightly on the door and waited to hear a reply before entering. Disturbing a wizard at work should be done with great caution.

He slipped in and shut the portal softly behind him. He then took stock of the situation.

A single bright light shone from a suspended ball, hovering with no visible wires in the middle of the room. It illuminated the body laid out on a modern-day gurney, wheeled cots being much easier to move around than the old-school stone altars the wizards used to prefer.

The room itself didn't have much in the way of modern medical equipment. No machines with beeping or flashing lights. Not even a fridge to store samples.

A counter ran along two of the walls and held an array of stands filled with glass vials and beakers. He also spotted a few small propane Bunsen burners; they had replaced the previous use of burning coal, which left a smoky residue on everything.

As for smell, nothing antiseptic permeated the air, nor did he scent death but rather a pleasant aroma of flowers, probably on account of the woman performing the autopsy being an elf. They tended to be finicky about their environments.

Dressed in a practical scrub suit, the elven lady leaned over the body on the table, hands hovering, not touching it.

Another woman, a human witch he'd met before, stood with pursed lips, watching.

"Elder Kell'en. Willow." Dale greeted them each in turn.

The elf didn't acknowledge him, but Willow's gaze met his, and she offered a faint smile. "Dale. I'm glad you're here. We started a few minutes early, but you haven't missed much."

"Sorry I'm late." The smooth tones of the vampire would have startled Dale if he'd not heard the door open. As it was, he didn't like knowing the bloodsucker stood behind him. Despite their kind having been under truce for centuries now, all Lycans had an innate distrust of vampires, which made him wonder even more how Pete did it.

Stepping aside, Dale made room for Anthony, the male Pete now shared a home with. A tall fellow, with classic features and blond hair. If not for his pallor, you'd never suspect what lurked within. Nor the fact that the vampire was centuries old yet appeared as if he were still in his late twenties.

"Now that we're all here, let's begin."

The elder, a wizard by training, an elf by birth, still hadn't chosen to look any of them in the eye. Damned elves were such snobs, and those who chose to follow the magical arts were the worst. But they sure knew how to throw a great hunt in the Summerlands.

Except the Summerlands were restricted now, most of the elves having withdrawn from the human world to their alternate space. A few chose to remain behind, mostly to act as ambassadors and eyes for the hidden elven court.

The audience remained quiet as the wizard—who did not answer to "sorceress," claiming it was sexist—began to speak.

"Victim is a male, thirty-seven Earth planetary rotations old, human in origin with trace amounts of elf in his lineage." All witches had something non-human in their blood, it was the reason they could do magic. "His body carries several charms. Basic ones," said with the slightest sneer. "One for his appearance meant to attract females, another to draw good luck, which seems to have failed, and one to warn him of danger. Again, not a very well-constructed charm."

"Gary was new to the coven and still learning how to use his powers," Willow commented.

"Perhaps Gary should have stuck to more mundane occupations. He'd probably be alive if he had."

As Willow's lips flattened, Dale felt a need to interject. "But if he had the capacity to do magic, then wouldn't a demon still be attracted?"

Bright sapphire eyes took a moment to peruse him. Thin lips pursed. "Much like the Lycan species, a demon finds its prey by scent. Had this human not chosen to indulge in things he only had a small knack for, he wouldn't have caused his magical scent to spike, thus not attracting the attention of whatever did this."

"Why do you say whatever?" Anthony, the lawyer, grabbed on to the word. "Isn't this a demon attack?"

"I'm not sure." Just saying the words caused Elder Kell'en to look as if she sucked a pile of lemons instead of just one.

"How can you not be sure? The evidence is very similar to the previous attacks."

"Similar, but not the same." The elder pointed. "While there are flesh and blood gone from the victim, the dentition is markedly different from the previous demon attacks."

"They're smaller."

"Smaller and improperly shaped. Let me show you." She waved her hand over a wound, and a ghostly image of it rose in the air. Waving her fingers around, manipulating the hovering picture, much like a person would use a mouse to work on a computer, she reverse engineered the bite to show the teeth that had left it.

Teeth that appeared—

"Those look awfully human," Willow noted.

Actually, they looked like a cross between human and Lycan, except his kind had pointed canines only. The hovering mold had pointed canines and a few jagged molars.

"What made those marks?" Anthony asked aloud.

"I don't know," grumbled Elder Kell'en. "I'll have to send some images to the Archivist." A sort of historian for all the crypto lore. "What I do know is whatever attacked this male wasn't alone." Waving her hand some more, she drew up some more bite marks, manipulating them to show the teeth that had left them.

Three different sets.

"Have we received the DNA analysis?" Despite all the magic they could access, science still played an important part in some things, like proper identification.

"The genetic marker test has not yet returned. There was a delay due to some cross contamination."

"What kind of contamination?" Anthony asked.

"Human." Said with a sneer. "We've scrubbed the labs and should have new results by tomorrow."

"What if it's not a mistake? Could someone human have done this?" Willow might have been the only one to say it, but Dale certainly wondered it.

"You better hope not," the elder said.

No kidding, because if there was something infecting humankind that caused them to attack magic users, then the whole world was in trouble. The elves, and their magical allies, would declare war to save themselves.

Chapter Eleven

Libraries weren't usually a place I hung out. Reading took too long. I mean, all those words. Ugh. All that effort felt like being in school again. When it came to literary bestsellers, I preferred to watch the television or big-screen adaptations.

Still, though, I doubted they'd make a story in the next hour that would explain what had happened in my town. I had questions about the Peabodys, their house, even the recent witch murders.

By now, I'd heard the word demon bandied about more than a few times. Demons, plus possessions.

You know what that means?

At last, the apocalypse had arrived. Shit was going to hit the fan.

Unless someone stopped it.

Someone like me.

Don't laugh. I could totally be heroine material—the brave, not the highly-addictive-injected-in-your-veins kind. I didn't fear facing danger. I'd been doing my Kegels religiously to hold on to that bladder if ever faced with pure evil.

I would fight. And, hopefully, not die.

Since staying alive seemed like a really good

plan, I thought it prudent to brush up on my demon lore—what they ate, were they hung like a horse or bigger, did they cooperate or submit, and could you decapitate them? Always good to know if it was worth the effort.

Since I didn't personally know any demons to ask my questions, I had to resort to a backup plan. What better place to find knowledge than the Internet—which I didn't currently have access to at my house, unless my phone counted. And let's be honest, major research on a teeny-tiny screen wasn't my idea of being a good sleuth. Add in the fact that my data package for my phone sucked, and I preferred to use a free Wi-Fi service.

While at the library, maybe I'd check into some books. Paper ones. Argh. Much as it pained me, the Internet only provided so much. I couldn't find any good stuff on the subject of demons that didn't involve a video game. None of my searches bore fruit either—*Search for demons eating faces? No, how about, I've been possessed.*

"No, I do not require mental service help, thank you very much, you smartass piece of technology." I glared at my phone.

It and the lovely world wide web had failed me.

I'd have to be intrepid and brave the paper cuts. In my new notepad—emblazoned with Hello Kitty—I'd take some stupendous notes of the things I discovered in dusty tomes made of skin written in a strange language that suddenly seemed so clear. Because of my mad research skills, I'd find the answers to fixing the apocalypse and save the day.

Not Scooby and his crew.

Me.

And to reward myself, I'd totally get a cat. A jab at my canine suitors, just like my shirt was a poke, considering it said, *Rub me to make me purr.*

No one had tried to yet, but the day was young. Sipping from my thermos where I'd smuggled in a mimosa, having drunk my limit of two at brunch, I spent a bit of time reading recent reports of the murders.

The human news didn't make any mention of demons or witches. They stuck to the basic facts as they knew them. Psycho kills person, police are baffled.

I had to wonder at the Lycans' and others' reluctance to admit the truth. The world knew about werewolves and mermaids and ogres, so why the hesitation over vampires coming out and telling humanity about demons?

Then again, if people knew about vampires and the fact that they could live forever, who was to say it wouldn't cause a frenzy? People were afraid of dying. I wouldn't put it past them to tie down a few vampires and start trying to dole out immortality to the masses. Even I could see that wouldn't end well.

As for demons, given the images I dug up from some ancient book—printed in the nineteen seventies in hardcover, not skin—I could see why no one wanted to believe they existed.

Demons were butt-ass ugly. As in even their mothers would never call them cute. Not even fugly.

The only attractive demon was probably a dead one that had been ashed into a pile of dust.

Despite the lack of actual pictures, the authors had nicely provided illustrations. Because art is sometimes subjective, they varied in depiction, some of the demons being shown as tall and wide, but there were short and skinny ones, too. Gnarly and knobby, smooth-skinned, and scaled. Some had tails or horns or both. Cloven hooves and claws. Their color differed, too, but they all had one thing in common.

According to all the books I read—*You want to know how many books that is?*

Technically one.

Blink.

Fine, maybe it was more like one that I skimmed for the main bits.

Blink. *Stop staring.* Sigh. *Fine. I looked at the pictures.*

The pictures were pretty graphic. Ugly. And violent. Demons killed.

They also liked eating flesh.

According to just about every religion—and movie once again, plus some boys named Winchester—they were pure evil. As in I wouldn't-want-to-meet-one-in-an-alley evil.

Shudder. Not one of fear but anticipation.

"Cold?" The query jolted me, but in a nice way, right between the thighs.

I know that voice. Had to love a voice that could caress your girl parts and make them all tingly.

I craned to peek over my shoulder and smiled at the good-looking man behind me. "Hello, Shaggy." I didn't hide the pleasure in my tone. Why would I when Sebastian looked as yummy as I recalled with his long hair held back, his green eyes dancing, and his lips curved in a smile?

A naughty smile. A smile that promised he'd do bad things—and that I'd enjoy them.

My va-jay-jay very much enjoyed that grin and thought I should drop my pants to smile back.

"Hey, baby, imagine meeting you in a place like this."

"Are you implying I can't read?" I tossed my hair. It was an adorable look. I knew because I'd practiced it in the mirror. It worked to perfection.

Sebastian looked horrified and hastened to explain. "Of course I think you can read. I'll bet you read tons."

"Then what were you implying, Shaggy?" I batted my lashes at him, innocent with a good dose of fuck-me-now. I didn't use this one often. I'd been saving it for a special occasion.

Sebastian's eyes glowed for a moment, a hint of wildness in their depths. Then his expression turned from jocular to stone cold.

"What I was trying to say is it's Sunday. I'd expect you anyplace but a library. Say, at home, maybe glossing your lips. Shaving the bush. Making dinner for a guy and changing the sheets. You know, the usual girl things."

The words held a hint of bitterness, and my

mouth rounded. "I don't believe they told you I made out with them." Then again, was I really surprised? Boys loved to brag.

"It might have come up," he said as he took the seat beside me.

"Are you jealous?" I leaned forward and put my hand on his knee.

He stiffened body-wise, but I couldn't tell if anything else did. Would he slap my hand away if I touched to see?

"Jealous of what? I heard you called their attempts at seduction *nice*." He smirked. "I guarantee that wouldn't happen with me."

"Are you daring me to kiss you?" As if I needed a challenge. Part of me wagged a mental finger and told me to stop. Playing with these three friends could drive a wedge. Did I want to cause trouble?

Well, yes, yes I did. And it would only be a problem if they insisted I choose one, and after last night's dream, I had a different idea in mind.

But could I convince them of it?

Here I was, getting ahead of myself. Planning a future with three guys when I'd yet to figure out if they'd like me past one date.

"I would never dare you to kiss me," Sebastian said, his hand atop mine on his leg, warm, heavy, and full of promise. "However, if you wanted to, I wouldn't say no."

"Naughty, Shaggy." Because, really, if I were Daphne, he was certainly the free-wheeling guy in this scenario. "I am supposed to be working."

"I know. I was watching you."

"You were?" I couldn't hide the surprised lilt. "Why did you wait so long before coming over to say hi?"

"I wasn't sure if you'd want me to. And then there was Dale—"

"Hold on a second." I narrowed my gaze. "Did Dale tell you to come babysit me?"

"Depends."

"On what?"

"If I say yes, does that mean you won't kiss me?"

Tossing my hair, I sniffed. "Who says I want to kiss you?"

"Your wet panties."

Damn these wolfmen and their keen sense of smell. "Maybe I just peed myself."

His lips twitched. "I can tell the difference, baby."

"Good for you. Despite my minor attraction to you, now is not the time," I said primly. Which surprised me. I didn't think I had any kind of prim and proper left in me. "We are in a library, and I'm busy." I also wished I'd worn some fake glasses and put my hair in a bun. I would wager Sebastian would have enjoyed the librarian look.

"I can see you're busy. All that research. That effort. You should take a break."

"No rest for the wicked." I might have licked my lips when I said it.

His nostrils flared. A beast barely held in check.

He tugged my hand higher up his thigh. Brazen, but exciting. His leg felt firm under my palm, the muscle in it thick and strong.

He murmured, "Have you found anything?"

Not yet, but if my hand kept moving, I'd bet it would find something erect.

Tempting. I did want to touch and see. But I shouldn't let him distract me. Things were rather complicated, and I had to tread carefully.

I snatched my hand away. "I haven't found anything interesting yet. Total bummer since I've been looking hard."

"And I'm feeling hard," was his wicked reply.

I turned to face him. "Are you going to keep making dirty jokes until I kiss you?"

"Probably."

"Won't Dale and Mike be pissed?"

He shrugged. "Let them. We had a pact to leave you alone. They broke it first."

"So is this a tit-for-tat thing?"

He leaned forward. "No, it's an I like you kind of thing. I liked you that first time we met."

"Yet you never called me after."

"Because I was told you were off-limits. Now, though, all bets are off. Give me a chance."

A chance to one-up his friends? A chance to make me come? A chance for me to find out if I preferred one over the others?

I asked him to, "Close your eyes."

He did, and I leaned forward, pressing my mouth lightly to his.

No surprise, I felt the same tingle as I had

with the other guys. The same burgeoning hunger and need.

My mouth slanted over Sebastian's, taking it more fully, sucking on his lower lip, feeling him respond.

The simple kiss turned into something with more panting and tongue. We ended up pressed tightly together, our lips meshed, his hands roaming, tugging me onto his lap.

Lucky me, I wore a skirt today, so when I straddled him, the core of me pressed against his jeans, a delightful friction.

Our spot in the back of the library gave us some privacy.

Some.

Yet even the thought of discovery couldn't cool my ardor. Rather, knowing someone could come across us added an element of...more. An erotic element.

His hands slid under my skirt to cup my ass cheeks. Our mouths were firmly meshed, and I moaned against his lips as he rocked me against the bulge in his pants.

I made a sound of disappointment when he manhandled me back into my seat.

"Don't worry, baby, we're not done." He winked before disappearing under the table.

His hands parted my knees, and his warm breath tickled the inside of my thighs. Surely, he wouldn't. Not here. Not...

"Oh." I couldn't help but exhale, and he whispered, "Shh," the sound vibrating against the moist crotch of my panties.

His mouth covered me again, teasing me with the fabric in the way, the heat of him making me squirm.

I bit my knuckle rather than cry out when he moved that scrap of fabric aside, baring me to the hot lash of his tongue.

Searing me with the heat of his mouth as he sucked my tender lips.

I trembled when he flicked my clit, the bud engorged and ready for more oral teasing.

He worked me with his tongue and lips, drawing jolts of pleasure, building up my excitement.

I leaned back in my seat, lost in the moment, so close to coming.

A finger slid into me, then another, while his tongue continued to lash my clit. My hips thrust against him, pushing his fingers deeper, my pleasure close to bursting.

He bit down on my swollen nub and sent me over the edge, the waves of my climax squeezing his fingers tights, the bliss of it rolling through me hard enough that my head fell back, my eyes closed, and I might have uttered a not so discreet, "Oh my God."

Someone took exception.

Chapter Twelve

"This is not a motel!" A shrill shriek. "Fornication is not allowed." The librarian stared down at me with stern disapproval. The best kind.

The rude interruption couldn't completely dispel my sexual languor. Opening my eyes slowly, as Sebastian yanked my skirt back in place, I drawled, "For the record, oral is not fucking." But it could feel just as good.

A snicker emerged from under the table before Sebastian did. He wore a very satisfied, smug grin. I probably wore the same one.

The librarian sucked in a breath, ready to breathe verbal brimstone on us.

Fun times.

"Sexual acts are not allowed here!" Said with the uptightness that came from a life spent alone with too many cats. Or so I surmised, given the cat hair coating the librarian's clothing.

The next smartass remark didn't come from me.

I know, surprising, hunh?

"Are you sure about the no-sex-acts thing?" Sebastian asked. "Because I've seen and read some of the books in your romance section. They do things in them that make even me blush. But, I should add, I'd be willing to try just about all of them." He winked.

The older woman, in her brown, button-up cardigan, her stern glasses, and wispy gray hair pulled tautly, pursed her thin lips. "Well, I never…"

"Obviously," he interjected, "or you'd have left us alone because you'd know how it feels to be so intrigued by a person that where you are doesn't matter. Only the need to seduce."

Okay, that went beyond panty wetting straight into take me right now, on this table, in plain sight of the librarian if she wouldn't leave.

Her arm extended and pointed. "It's time you left."

What a surprise, another place I got kicked out of.

"I can't leave yet. I wasn't done researching." I pointed to my pile of books. Not a single comic book among them.

"You are done, missy." Said with a strange glee.

It was then I noticed something about the old lady. Something amiss, and I didn't mean the fact that the buttons weren't matching up properly on her sweater or that one earring was missing, but the fact that her eyes glowed. A pinprick of red in the center of the pupils.

I'd seen that before, and recently, too. At least I knew better than to eat any offered cookies.

Standing up, I confronted the librarian. "Have you recently come into contact with any evil artifacts or participated in any Satanic rituals?"

"What kind of craziness is this?" she hissed.

"Baby, what are you doing?" muttered Sebastian.

I waved a hand to shush him. "Did you inherit a ring or buy a mirror from an estate auction?"

"Get out."

"By any chance, are you acquainted with the Peabodys?"

Her lip curled. "Who I know is none of your business."

"Are you, or aren't you?"

"And if I am?"

The red light in her eyes got brighter, which prompted me to say, "Are you possessed?"

At that, Sebastian jumped from his seat and began to stack the books. "Sorry, ma'am, we'll just be heading off now…"

His words trailed off, probably because the librarian, much like Mr. Peabody, floated above the floor.

"Um, baby, what's happening."

"I think we found a clue!" I clapped my hands in delight, even if I didn't know what it meant.

"The darkness is coming," she intoned in a deep voice that reverberated, raising the hairs on my skin. I really needed to make that appointment to wax them.

The red light in the librarian's eyes vanished on account that they'd rolled back in her head, leaving only the whites behind. Which, I will add, wasn't exactly an improvement on her appearance.

"Oh, shit," Sebastian muttered. "This can't be good."

"I knew it. She's possessed." And I'd found her! I was rocking this case.

"*She*," enunciated the librarian, "is hungry."

Now where had I heard that before? Suddenly, I was everyone's meal of choice.

"Sorry, but the kitchen is closed." I crossed my arms over my chest and shook my head. I'd already fed a werewolf today. I wasn't about to feed this woman.

My answer didn't go over well. The librarian's mouth opened wide, and a whistling scream came out of it.

Cool. It would have been cooler with wasps, though.

Sebastian wasn't as intrigued. He grabbed me by the hand and pulled. "We should go."

"Go?" I leaned against his tugging. "But we just found a clue to the Peabody case."

"Yeah, and she's not happy about it."

The librarian spun in the air, arms outstretched, head back, the noise from her mouth not diminishing, not fading even to take a breath.

The rapid turning caused wind to whip up, not exactly a normal occurrence inside a building. Even though we were huddled in the back, people in the library noticed.

It didn't take long before the first person appeared between the stacks with a smart phone raised, taking a video. Soon, there was a handful, muttering amongst themselves, unsure what to think of the librarian flipping out mid-air.

I did hear a few comments along the lines of "someone must be filming either a movie or a prank." *The Ring* had done something epic when their third installment came out. The looks on people's faces when that girl crawled out of the televisions in that store was to die for.

Currently, no one looked too scared. Nothing bad had happened. A bit of wind, an annoying shriek, and yet still, Sebastian tugged at my arm.

"Baby, I really don't think we should stick around."

"Don't tell me you're a pussy. I thought you were a wolf. Aren't wolves super brave?"

He sighed. "I am, but even we know when to run. This"—he indicated the spinning old lady—"is a run away moment because this involves magic, and neither of us is equipped to deal with that."

How could he not be equipped? He was a fucking Lycan. "Can't you just eat her?"

"In public, with people watching?" Sebastian gave a pointed look to the gawkers with their phones live streaming before facing me again.

Hmm. Good point.

Still, the idea of leaving didn't appeal. This was the moment I'd trained for, and I felt ready to face the forces of darkness. If only I'd brought a decent weapon. "I am going to have to find a bigger purse," I muttered as I grabbed my stuff and shoved it into my satchel.

"A bigger purse for what?" he asked, pulling me along the outskirts, his gaze fixated on

Spinerella—a name the librarian surely deserved given her long skirt flared slightly during her spins, and her hair, now unbound, floated around her head.

"I need a bigger purse for my machete. All the movies and books agree that chopping off the head usually solves the problem."

That earned me a startled glance.

"And how would you explain a decapitation to the cops?" he asked.

Such an oddly practical question coming from him. I wrinkled my nose. "Self-defense against the dark arts."

"That's not an actual thing."

It isn't? Dammit, there I went mixing up my Harry Potter lore with the real world again.

We'd almost made it to the corridor of books that would give us a straight shot out of there when Spinerella stopped screaming.

It wasn't as reassuring as you'd think, especially since she said, "Oh, Brenda, Mrs. Peabody says to ask how you liked her cookies."

I halted in my tracks and whirled long enough to say, "Tell her I prefer store-bought."

Wrong answer.

Spinerella swooped and flew toward us, crazy white eyes glaring, mouth open wide, and fingers crooked into claws.

All of a sudden, I didn't need encouragement to run.

Ever see the movies where the books start flying out, and the shelves topple over?

It didn't happen. *I know, major disappointment.*

We popped out of the stacks into the reception area with the desk to check books in and out, freedom only yards away, when something grabbed me from behind.

By grab, I meant the crazy librarian dug her nails in and lifted me while cackling.

"Yummy, yummy in my tummy," the crazy bitch sang.

"Ouch," I yelled as I thrashed my legs.

"Hold on, baby. I'll save you." Sebastian didn't ditch me to Spinerella. He wrapped his arms around my legs and tried to work as an anchor.

Leaning back, he strained with all his weight to bring me back to the floor, but the damned possessed librarian kept lifting.

Holy shit, she was strong. So strong that I wondered how I'd escape. Would I become the next victim? Would my picture be in the newspaper?

Adorable Brenda Whittaker Sadly Succumbed to a Nefarious Force. Or would it be more along the lines of, *Dumb Blonde Should have Run Faster.*

Our ascent abruptly halted as another body suddenly threw themselves on Sebastian. And then another grabbed on to him.

Only with all that combined weight did Spinerella let me go, and I landed in a heap on top of three men.

My men.

How nice of them to provide a muscled landing. Did they have to ruin it with matching scowls?

Before I could say anything, I found myself

dumped onto the floor, face first on dirty tile.

What happened to my pile of men?

Rolling, I saw them standing over me, Dale, Mike and Sebastian, and holy shit, things had just gotten hot. As in fantasy come to life hot because they were taking off their shirts.

I caught the fabric they dropped, hugging the warm material to me, smelling them on it. I just wished they'd turn around so I could see their fronts. Their muscled backs and tight asses in those jeans were fabulous, but I wanted to see the goods.

But this was where the fantasy fell apart. They weren't stripping to tease and please me. According to the hair sprouting from their backs, the way the musculature and bones in their bodies shifted, they were going into wolfman mode.

Still rather fascinating.

I scrambled to my feet and noted that they faced off against a hovering Spinerella, her eyes still white as snow, her lips the bright red of blood, the stain of it dripping down her chin.

A sobbing person held a hand to his neck while another supported him screaming, "Call an ambulance."

It appeared I was off the menu, as a hungry Spinerella had chosen to snack on someone else.

Oh, hell no. This was supposed to be my gig.

Dumping the shirts, I pushed my way between furry bodies, or meant to. They kept shoving me behind them.

"Stay still," growled Dale. A real growl this

time.

"Don't make me eat you," snarled Mike.

"Sebastian already did." I never could keep my mouth shut.

Two shaggy heads swiveled, and Sebastian, despite his muzzle, managed to smirk. "She was delicious."

Because I didn't like the smugness in his tone or expression, I couldn't help but add, "It was nice."

More conversation on that topic would have to wait. Spinerella took that moment to dive at us, and by us, I meant me.

She still likes me best!

She swooped over their heads, hands outstretched for yours truly.

Wishing once again I had my machete, I had to make do. I threw a book. A big book, a Stephen King one with lots of weight that she batted aside, but it proved distraction enough for Dale to spring up and grab the librarian by the legs.

Then Mike was in there, too, holding an arm while Sebastian grabbed the other.

I didn't quite know what they expected to do, pull on her until she split? Kind of gross, but hey, if it worked, I wouldn't knock it.

A warm breeze suddenly brushed past me, smelling of springtime flowers and green grass. A voice, deep and resonant, uttered, "Sleep."

One word. One disappointing word that made me yawn, and Spinerella went limp and would have collapsed except my trio of wolfmen caught her and lay her down on the floor.

A curiosity to know who had spoken had me turning around. I glimpsed a man, tall and gray-haired, the strands pulled back into a ponytail, his features sharp, his attitude cocky judging by his smirk. He wore a slate-gray suit with a mauve shirt.

"You can unhand the female," he declared, waving his hand most pompously. "She's harmless now."

"Show off," muttered a very pretty redhead, who pushed past him.

"It's not showing off, it's merely a standard skill for a true magical practitioner," he replied as the woman made her way slowly to the librarian's side.

"A sleep dart would have worked just as well and drawn less attention," the redhead sniped. "Or have you forgotten there is still an audience around?"

"Not for long." The man in the suit did some strange thing with his fingers and said a few low words before sweeping his hands out and shouting, "Be gone!"

The people who remained gawking suddenly got moving, rushing for the doors. I almost followed. My feet even took a step, but I shook it off.

The action was here, which meant I would remain.

The auburn-haired woman had reached the fallen librarian, and yet she didn't touch her, choosing instead to circle around before saying, "Are you sure the spell you cast worked, Morfeus?"

"Are you questioning me, hearth witch?" The disdain in his tone couldn't have been clearer.

"There's something wrong with her aura." The woman crouched a few feet away and frowned at the now sleeping Spinerella.

"Obviously, her aura is tainted," Morfeus said snottily. "She is possessed like the other fellow in the sanatorium. Or had you not noticed she showed some of the same traits?"

"You mean the floating and wanting to eat people thing." I spoke, and yet Morfeus acted as if I hadn't, striding past me to crouch by Spinerella.

He waved his hand over her face, the edges of it glowing yellow.

I wasn't the only one to visibly start when her eyes opened wide, the red glow in them back and more pronounced. Her lips stretched, wide, then wider still, displaying some awfully large and jagged teeth.

The librarian cackled, and not in a nice old lady kind of way. "Silly little wizard. Thinks he can put me to sleep."

"Foul creature inhabiting this body, remove yourself at once."

Spoken with the right degree of imperialism, but the thing possessing the woman remained unimpressed.

"You don't have the power to remove me. I've tasted Wiccan blood. I'm stronger now. Too strong for the likes of you to cast out."

"We shall see about that." He held out his hand, and it began to glow white.

I was probably the only one who said

"oooh" in a delighted way when an impossibly long tongue emerged from her mouth to lick his palm.

"Smells so yummy. Yummier than a witch. I think I shall have wizard for supper."

Before Morfeus could recoil, Spinerella grabbed him and went for his neck.

The wizard dude bellowed, and I might have shrieked—in excitement because, holy shit, I had a live-action horror movie happening in front of me.

The redhead looked appalled.

"Do something!" Dale barked, growled, or whatever it was he did in wolfman form. I could understand him, but he had a definite Lycan accent.

"I don't know what to do," she said. "My teachings didn't cover this."

My movies, on the other hand, did. I grabbed hold of the letter opener on the desk and ran with a scream at the librarian.

I was caught before I made it two steps. "Let me at her!" I yelled, waving around my eight-inch sword.

Mike held me as Sebastian and Dale went to rescue the wizard dude, who didn't look so snooty anymore with someone snacking on his neck. They tackled her, ripping her off the guy.

I had to give him props. Despite the pain, and the blood, the wizard stood up and snarled, "Move aside or share her fate!"

Apparently, this was one dude you didn't want to ignore. Dale and Sebastian dove away, leaving Spinerella standing alone, her lips covered in blood, her eyes glowing with madness.

As she smiled, her teeth dripping red, she screeched, "Time for dessert."

The wizard thrust out his hands and muttered something guttural—and three-quarters gibberish I was sure—and an orange ball of fire formed in front of him.

Pretty.

That momentary elation lasted only until the ball Morfeus flung hit an opaque shield the demon held up at the last moment. The fireball got flung back!

"Duck!" someone shouted.

The shit disturber in kindergarten, I always yelled "goose" just to cause chaos. I didn't get a chance this time because Mike smooshed me to the floor.

The fireball singed overhead and hit the stone columns alongside the doors. It caused a tremble in the building.

It also made a certain Spinerella cackle. "Miss me, miss me, now you have to feed me."

"Hearth witch, make yourself useful," barked the wizard.

I heard more guttural chanting, joined by a more tentative female voice. It reached a crescendo, and something in the air prickled my skin. Even with my face pressed down, I could see a red glow at the edges of my vision. A big fireball that Mike wouldn't roll over to let me see.

Whoosh. I could practically hear it burn the air as it was launched, and the librarian screeched.

"You might win today, but we are—"

Splat. She never got to finish her speech as meat chunks rained down on us.

Gross.

Standing, Mike held out a hand to help me up, his wolfman gone again, his bare upper body splattered in red but not as covered in guts as Sebastian and Dale. Their fur stood in goopy spikes with the amount they had absorbed.

I wrinkled my nose. "You both need a bath." Actually, we all did. I clapped my hands and rounded on Morfeus. "Dude, that was epic. I mean, I was a little worried when that first fireball got tossed back, but you pulled through with the help of Red over there. Good job." I finished with more clapping and a whistle of appreciation.

"Who is this annoying female?" the wizard snapped.

"Who are you?" I fired back. I knew his name, and the whole wizard bit, but what was he? I didn't get the impression he was entirely human.

Striking electric blue eyes focused on me. "None of your business, *human*."

And with a snap of his fingers, I passed out.

Sebastian Interlude

Sebastian caught Brenda before she hit the floor. He shot a glare at the man responsible.

"What the fuck is your problem, asshole?" He wasn't the only one pissed.

Mike and Dale stood shoulder-to-shoulder, their fur having receded, and yet even in their flesh, they provided a shield between the newcomer and Brenda.

Morfeus's lips curled. "Isn't this cute, litter pups standing together. Why don't you go fetch a bone and let the grownups take care of this situation?"

"Why you—" Dale held Sebastian back.

But Dale wasn't about to let the wizard pull his shit. "Do you call this taking care of the situation?" He gestured to the gore sprayed all around them.

"Would you have preferred I let the creature get loose?"

"How about containing it so we could study it?" Mike countered.

"Because your studies have helped so much," the wizard mocked. "I know about your case at the sanatorium. The one now locked in a padded room."

Mike's lips pressed tight. "At least he's still alive."

"And useless since he can't answer any questions."

"She can't answer any either, but now we're going to have to deal with the human authorities because you just had to make her go splat. We can't hide this." Dale had on his big boss face, giving orders, sounding all firm. It made Sebastian want to say something totally inappropriate.

But this might not be the right time.

"We couldn't exactly let that *thing*"— Morfeus sneered—"loose. Imagine the havoc it would have caused."

"We could have tried containment first."

Sebastian kind of agreed with Morfeus when he said, "You can't imprison every problem. Some are too dangerous."

Willow rolled her eyes. "Would you guys knock it off? We should be working together."

"Working together to clean up his mess?" Dale snorted. "Why should I?"

Sebastian knew the answer to this one, but Willow answered first. "You are currently implicated, given you're presently doused in guts, and people saw you wolfing out."

"I'm going to have you all brought up on indecent werewolf exposure charges," Morfeus declared.

"Good luck with that. There won't be any witnesses if I eat you." Body poised for battle, Dale snarled the threat.

"This bickering isn't helping," snapped

Willow. "Stop it."

Morfeus smirked. "You should listen to the hearth witch."

"Would you stop it with that hearth witch shit." With her eyes flashing, Willow rounded on Morfeus. "I have had enough of your shit. My name is Willow. And I am just about as happy as you are to be working with you."

"This is an insult," sneered the wizard. "Pairing me with the likes of you."

"The likes of me isn't intimidated by you." She leaned forward, hands on her hips.

"You should be." Morfeus pressed his lips tightly together in disapproval.

"Who is the douchebag?" Dale asked with a glower at the man, who ignored them in favor of flicking chunks of flesh off his suit.

Waving her hand, Willow managed a very sarcastic, "This pompous ass is apparently the grand Whizziar they put in charge of the demon investigation."

"No apparently about it, hearth witch. I am in charge. And a good thing, too, given the mess you're all making."

"You're one to talk about messes," grumbled Dale.

Sebastian chose to keep quiet. Some things weren't worth getting his head shrunk for.

"I thought the college of wizards had no interest in coming out to the world quite yet," Mike noted.

"We don't."

"Yet you're flinging magic around," Mike

reiterated. "Killing civilians."

"I removed a problem."

"And made a bigger one. You can't hide what happened here. People were taking pictures and videos."

"This might be difficult for your dog-sized brains to comprehend, but the first thing I did before entering was erect a containment field, which, as soon as the humans crossed, erased not only their memories of the last hour but also wiped their phones of everything. No video, no proof, no scandal."

"Some live feeds will have made it out before you arrived," Sebastian noted.

"We are not new when it comes to containment. My team is already working on it."

"Even if you erase everything, they'll still talk."

"Talk isn't proof. And this conversation bores me." The wizard turned away, but Sebastian still had a question.

"What did you do to Brenda?" She remained limp in his arms.

"Merely put the girl to sleep. I can't abide noisy women."

"On account they're probably—usually— telling you what an ass you are?" Willow remarked.

"Be silent, hearth witch."

"Stuff it, asswipe. I don't take orders from you. I agreed to cooperate with the wizard collective only because the coven doesn't know how to defend against this ongoing threat. But accepting your help doesn't mean you get to be a douche nozzle to me, or anyone else you think is beneath you."

"I don't think you are beneath me. I know you are." Said in a tone that said he really wanted to get punched out.

"For a guy with the snooty airs of an elf, you don't look like an elf," Sebastian remarked.

"Probably had his ears docked. Betcha his parents are proud. Not," said Dale with a smirk.

"He's obviously got small-penis syndrome," Mike diagnosed. "Care to wager he drives an overpriced sports car?"

The grand Whizziar might have flushed red. His eyes certainly narrowed. "I will have you all brought up on charges."

"Of what?" Dale said, still smirking. "Deflating your sizeable ego?"

"Interfering in a collective investigation."

Dale looked between Sebastian and Mike. "We had no idea the library was such a hot spot for demon possessions."

"Then you haven't been paying attention. We are actually dealing with a minor epidemic. But it shouldn't take us long to get it under control."

"You mean there's more of this shit"—he gestured to the meaty entrails dripping down the walls— "happening around town?"

Willow answered. "We've been getting calls since last night. A few employees in the firehouse began to display odd characteristics. And a policeman, too."

"Any idea why service personnel are being affected?"

She shrugged. "Not a clue. It doesn't seem to be contagious at this point. And if caught early on, we can actually expel whatever it is causing them to change."

"I'm sure it will be something they ate." The grand Whizziar waved a hand and sniffed. "They're human. They probably forgot to wash their hands first."

Ignoring the wizard, Dale spoke to Willow. "Need some help? The pack is involved at this point and willing to offer our services."

The witch shook her head. "You're already helping enough."

"While you're all yapping, you do realize we're standing in the middle of a carnage scene?" Mike remarked. "I don't know about you, but I don't think it would be healthy for any of us to be found covered in this woman's guts."

The distant wail of sirens punctuated his remarks.

"If you would all depart, I will ensure there's nothing for the human authorities to find," remarked the grand Whizziar.

"We can't exactly walk around like this," Dale observed, skimming a hand up and down to showcase his blood-covered body.

"That is simple enough to fix." Willow hummed something sweet and soft then made an odd gesture in each of their directions, each twist and wave of her hands somehow dryly sluicing off the grime from their skin and clothes.

She finished with a slashing movement that cleared a path on the floor to walk on. "Try not to touch anything on your way out."

"And hurry it up. We don't have much time to cleanse," sniped Morfeus.

"How do you plan to clean this up in the next two minutes?" Which was about how long they had before those sirens arrived.

"There is only one thing that will cleanse this place." A ball of orange fire formed in the wizard's palm. "Unless you want to be cleansed, as well, take your human cargo and move along." Morfeus waved a hand.

"You're just going to cremate the librarian?" Dale said, his tone a touch incredulous. "What about her family? Friends?"

"She's no longer your concern."

When Dale might have argued, Willow shook her head. Usually a spitfire, if she advocated silence, then they should listen.

Still carrying Brenda, Sebastian waited until they were outside to say, "That dude is in serious need of an attitude adjustment."

"I agree, but if even Willow's holding her tongue, then chances are he's some hotshot we shouldn't fuck with."

"He's a sociopath. He'd kill us in the blink of an eye," Mike stated.

"And this is the guy they've got running an investigation?" Dale snorted. "Maybe they're not so keen on cover-up after all."

"Dude is a total asshat, but Willow's pretty nice." Sebastian might be enamored with Brenda, but he wasn't blind.

"Willow's the exception. Most witches don't

like Lycans." Dale led the way to a giant truck that Sebastian instantly coveted.

The psychiatrist of their group felt a need to add his learned two cents. "It's not that they don't like Lycans. It's more the fact that their cats go ballistic around us."

"So that talk about them having cats is true?" Sebastian asked. He'd only recently learned about the witches around them. They tended to be secretive.

"Very true. Witches require a familiar to help ground them when they cast spells. While any animal can technically fill that spot, felines are the most receptive for magic and the least likely to interrupt a casting."

Dale snared Brenda's satchel, which Sebastian had thought to grab along with her. He rummaged inside for keys. Keys to the blessed blue truck.

"Is this beautiful beast hers?" Sebastian asked, gaping in delight.

"Yup. And she drives like a maniac when she gets behind the wheel."

"My kind of girl," Sebastian remarked.

"All of our kind of girl. You're lucky we don't punch you out for making a move on her."

"Competition is healthy."

"Not if it breaks your jaw," Dale retorted. "I sent you to the library to watch over her, not smother your face in her crotch."

He shrugged. "I'm a dog. What did you expect?"

Sebastian deposited Brenda on the

passenger side, noting the lack of a proper back seat.

"I'll drive." He held out his hand for the keys, but Dale gave him a side-eye.

"No, I'll drive. You'll ride with Mike and—"

Boom. Looking back, they noted the flames shooting out of the library, their brightness momentarily illuminating the ground where Whizziar and the witch were standing out front.

A billow of smoke obscured them, and when a gust of wind cleared it away, they were gone.

And they should leave, too. Shirtless men, with an unconscious woman in their custody, were bound to draw the wrong kind of attention.

Sebastian headed for the passenger side of the car. "Let's roll."

"We'll meet you at her place," Mike added in Dale's direction.

"We don't all need to be there."

But Mike wouldn't let Dale dictate to them. "Yes, we do all have to be there. It's time she decided who she wants."

"What if she can't?" Sebastian asked.

"A better question is, can we share?" Dale's question hung in the air.

The query preyed on Sebastian as he caught a ride with Mike.

To his credit, Mike remained silent and waited for Sebastian to speak first.

"Would sharing one girl be so bad?" he asked.

Mike cast him a look. "You'd be okay with us taking turns?"

"Sure." Sebastian shrugged. "Don't forget, unlike you guys, after my dad died, Mom hooked up with Kent and Harold. Best thing that could have happened to her, and to me." They'd given him twice the dad to make up for the one he'd lost. "For me, the concept of more than one man for a woman isn't so weird, and in many cases, it works."

"It seems weird to me," Mike said and then sighed. "Yet, at the same time, if I had to share a woman with anyone, who better than my best friends? When you think of it, it's ideal. We've been living together since college. If we each were to find a different woman, we'd probably have to move into separate places."

"Split up the three amigos?" Sebastian inhaled sharply. "But we're a team."

"A team for extracurricular activities and work. We've never extended that to the bedroom."

"But you're thinking of it," Sebastian prodded, not about to let Mike change the thread of this conversation.

"A little."

Noting a hint of red in his features, Sebastian laughed. "Holy shit, bro, you're serious. You've been thinking of it, in a dirty way."

"No." The ruddy color heightened.

"Dude, nothing wrong with wanting a threesome, or a foursome."

"That's just it. I don't really want it. At least, not in a way that involves touching you or Dale."

"I hear a but."

"But I can see the erotic possibilities. Just watching would provide tons of titillation."

"Mike, you dog, you're a voyeur."

The redness in his buddy's cheeks didn't fade, and he wouldn't look at Sebastian. "Tell anyone, and I'll slip you a drug that makes your penis limp."

"Dude, that's just mean. And who would I tell? On the contrary, knowing you're cool with it means when we get Brenda into bed—"

"If."

"When." Sebastian was just that confident about where things were heading. "Nothing wrong with a little fantasy, bro. However, knowing you like to watch, I'm going to have to make sure I give a top-notch performance. Wouldn't want to let you down."

He grabbed Mike's thigh and squeezed then laughed as his friend slammed his fist down on his own leg as Sebastian snatched his hand away.

"No touching."

Sebastian laughed. "If you insist, but given the size of my junk, don't blame me if my dick gets in your way or if it touches yours when I sink balls deep while she's blowing you." The length of his dick made that a possibility.

"Tag teaming her does sound exciting," Mike admitted.

"And I promise, it will feel even better."

Chapter Thirteen

I felt wondrously rested, if confused, when I woke up in my bed, face plastered to the pillow, drooling like a fiend.

Lifting my head, I shrieked when a voice said, "How you feeling?"

Not violated, that was for sure. Then again, that was probably a good thing. I'd want to be awake for it.

Rolling over in bed, I noticed Mike sitting in a chair, the pile of clothes I kept on it moved to make him some room.

The urge to run fingers through my hair, throw myself on my back, and beckon him wantonly warred with my pasty mouth, sweaty thighs, and urge to pee.

Hard to be sexy when your bladder threatened to wet the bed.

"What happened? How did I get here?"

"We brought you home."

"We?" As in a trio of wolves. How exciting.

"All of us have been taking turns watching you."

"Afraid I'll run off?"

"Actually, we were more concerned about you showing signs of possession."

"Sorry to break it to you, but the crazy in here"—I tapped my head—" is all mine."

"You're not crazy."

"You say that, and yet you don't like me." I could tell I'd thrown him off guard.

"What makes you say that?"

"Well, you never smile around me for one."

He scowled. "I'm not a smiley kind of guy."

"You never called after our make-out session."

"I've been busy."

"And now you're making excuses." My lips turned down. "You can tell me, you know. I can handle it. You wouldn't be the first guy to not like me, and I am sure you won't be the last."

"Why do you care what I think?"

"I don't know, which I guess is a whole other ballgame. Let me ask you, since you're a psych doctor, maybe you can explain to me why it is I seem to scare most people off."

"You haven't scared Chloe away."

"She's the exception, not the rule."

"It's not unusual for a woman your age to date and discard different partners."

"If I was doing the discarding, perhaps it wouldn't bother me so much." I squirmed as some of my inner vulnerability peeked out. I wasn't usually given to introspective depression.

"Perhaps if you toned down your more outrageous outbursts."

My lips turned down. "You mean change who I am for other people?"

"Yes." He said it, and then a moment later

changed it to, "No. You shouldn't have to change who you are because there's nothing wrong with you."

"Is that your professional opinion?" I asked with a smile.

"There's nothing wrong with being headstrong or outspoken."

"Unless you're a girl looking for a man who won't run off the first time I scream 'holy fuck' in a movie theatre when there's a good twist."

A smile pulled his lips. "I can see how some people might find it embarrassing."

"Would you?"

"Yes." He didn't even try to lie. "But do you know who would totally enjoy that? Sebastian."

I blinked at him. Did he just throw his buddy at me? Did this mean he wasn't interested?

Utterly confusing.

And I told him so. "Is this your way of saying you don't want to be with me?"

He recoiled, his expression quite startled. "No. I mean. Um. That is. I , um, like you."

He stammered. Mr. Grumpy Pants *stammered*. Maybe he wasn't as cool and collected as I thought. Might I even say he was definitely still interested?

"Let me see if I understand. You like me, but think I should go to the movies with Sebastian."

"Not all the time."

"But some of the time, and you'd do this even knowing I like to fool around at the movies?"

I questioned.

"I would send you with him, yes, because I'm not into public sex." My lips turned down until he added, "But I am not completely without adventure. My office has a lock and a sturdy desk."

My mouth rounded. "Okay, that I wasn't expecting." I smiled. "But I like it."

"Mike!" Dale bellowed for him, and he sighed.

"I'd better go see what he wants."

"He'd better want to order some food because I'm starving. I'm going to hop in the shower, and by the time I get out, there'd better be something I can put in my mouth."

"I'll find you something for your mouth."

Did Mike just make a dirty joke? "The kind of thing I can chew on."

"Chew, spit, or swallow. Completely up to you." Said utterly deadpan.

I narrowed my gaze on him. This other side of Mike intrigued me. But my stomach demanded satisfaction. "Food, or I won't be responsible for my behavior." People who knew me understood what happened if I wasn't fed.

"I'll let him know," Mike said, almost smiling.

I'd crack that baby yet.

I admired his ass as he left the room before hopping out of bed and stretching.

My shoulders ached, and when I stripped off my shirt, not the same one I'd been wearing at the library, I noticed the gouges in them, bruised crescents where Spinerella had grabbed me.

What I couldn't figure out was, why? Why me? And what was the connection to the Peabodys?

A hot shower didn't help me puzzle it out but did leave me feeling human. Very human. Also very horny.

I'd almost died. I think. Who knew what the possessed librarian wanted from me. It was an interesting change that I'd gone from too few people wanting me to too many.

Whatever is a girl to do.

How about three men?

When I exited the bathroom, freshly showered after the library incident—which ended in a meaty bang that thrilled the horror lover in me—I found the guys still arguing.

Not wrestling naked to see who would win me.

Not trying to figure out who'd get the damned pizza I needed to feed my hungry belly.

Nor were they using their anger to clean my apartment, which sadly needed a good vacuum.

Since I wasn't in the mood to yell but did want a spot of quiet, I did what any woman in a robe would do.

I flashed them.

Held that robe open long enough to draw all their eyes, drop their jaws—stoking my ego—and blessed silence descended.

I then hid the goods because, hello, "Where's the food?"

"That's all you have to say?" Dale snapped.

"How can you ask about food after what

happened?"

I rolled my eyes. "It's not like I asked for steak tartare." Even my stomach rebelled at the idea. "But would it have killed you guys to order a pizza?"

Knock. Knock.

We all looked at the door, a door Mike crossed the room to answer.

He handed some cash to the delivery guy and then whirled around with several boxes.

I clapped my hands. "You are totally my favorite person right now."

"Don't I get brownie points for planning to bring food over later?" Dale retorted. "Along with the beer you demanded."

"How come you invited him and not me?" Sebastian pouted.

"Plates or napkins?" Mike asked. He plopped the boxes on my living room table, and I sat down cross-legged in front of it. Realized silence had fallen again and adjusted my robe.

Over a slice of pepperoni with extra cheese, I asked, "So, am I to assume that, given the sudden attack at the library"—aimed at me, giddy inner dance—"that I'm now under your protection again?"

"You are not to leave this apartment." Guess who uttered that imperial decree.

"That's not going to fly. I have to work tomorrow."

"Call in sick."

"Mike, I'm shocked at you. Advising me to lie." I shook my head.

"Think of it as playing hooky," Sebastian offered.

"I'll be bored."

"Better bored than dead." Dale had no sense of humor.

"You really think one of Spinerella's possessed friends will come attack me at work?" I should be so lucky.

"They're not who I'm most worried about," Dale muttered ominously.

"What Dale means to say is, if you were to talk about what's happened to you lately, you could end up an unwilling patient in my care." Mike threw that out there before taking a big bite of his meat lover's.

"Are you saying if I don't behave you'll institutionalize me?" My query had an incredulous note.

"If I have to. Even you'd have a hard time getting in trouble in a padded room."

"I'm not crazy," I grumbled. Horny, perhaps a little stupid where danger was concerned, and eating way too much in front of guys I found hot, but definitely not loony bin material.

"Why don't you tell her the real truth?" Sebastian said before taking a bite.

"What truth? What aren't you telling me?"

Dale glared at Sebastian, as did Mike, which meant this was going to be juicy.

"Spill it," I demanded. "I have a right to know."

"Unfortunately, the incident at the library brought you to the attention of the grand

Whizziar."

"What's a grand whizzer?"

"Whizziar," Mike enunciated. "He's a fellow high up in the wizard collective."

"Wizards." I snickered. Some things still had the ability to tickle my inner princess who dreamed of knights and dragons.

"You shouldn't laugh about this. Morfeus isn't a person to trifle with from what we've learned."

"You mean the dude I met at the library? I didn't get the impression he liked me." No surprise there.

"He doesn't like most humans, and he especially dislikes humans who know more than they should."

"What's the big deal? So what if I know magic exists? I'm pretty sure the whole world knows by now."

"Actually, the collective and the TDCM did an excellent job of covering up the incident at the library."

"How the hell did they cover up the fact that Spinerella—"

"Who?"

"Crazy possessed librarian chick. Duh." I rolled my eyes. "How could they hide what she did and what the grand whizzer did to stop her?"

"Easy. He wiped the minds of the witnesses. Cleared their phones, and burnt the library down."

"He did what?" I might not love books, but even I was shocked.

"Burnt it, eradicating all trace evidence, and the human authorities are treating the few witness claims that escaped Morfeus's net as hallucinations brought on by the gas leak in the library that caused the explosion."

I blinked. "Do you mean to say instead of admitting demons and wizards exist, they fabricated a ginormous lie? Am I the only one who thinks they're nuts? Why not just come out of their closet, or hat, or whatever wizards hide in? Lycans and mermaids did it. What's the big deal?"

"The big deal is that the collective is an old institution that has made it past all the witch burnings and the Inquisition, and survived this long because of rules. Rules, I might add, that the Lycans broke when they went public."

"Boy, were they pissed," Sebastian exclaimed.

"They were livid," Dale agreed. "But they couldn't take it back once it was out there. And they couldn't stop the other races that decided to join us. Not everyone was happy with the strict rules governing our existence."

"So a bunch of you rebelled against the wizard overlords." A statement that deserved a giggle. "Still not sure why that endangers my life. I mean, Chloe knows about magic and witches and vampires, and they're not trying to erase her ass."

"Because she was formally claimed by both Pete and Anthony, which assured her safety. The wizards can't touch her unless they want to start a war with the Lycans and vampire clans."

"So what you're saying is if someone claims

my butt, I'll be safe."

"Essentially." Said rather faintly, and it was then I noticed the men staring at anything but me.

The sharp pang of hurt lifted my chin. "I see. None of you want to do that."

"We didn't say that," Dale hastened to say.

"And yet none of you volunteered."

"I will." Sebastian raised his hand.

Mike slapped it down. "No one is doing anything yet. Claiming is a serious thing and not to be done lightly."

"What is it, like marriage or something?" Surely not, because if Chloe had gotten married, she would have told me, not to mention we had wedding binders—shoved in a drawer gathering dust in my case. As for Chloe's, I was supposed to be her maid of honor, and we'd both planned to wear steel-toed work boots so we could take awesome pics with the photographer.

"Claiming is more binding than marriage. There's no divorce from it. No walking away. It's for life."

"Damn. No wonder none of you want to commit. Who'd want to be chained to me for life?" A laugh bubbled from me, edged with a note I didn't like. A note of bitterness. As if I'd let them hurt me. "Well, it's been nice, boys. But I think it's time you left."

"We're not leaving," stated Dale.

"We should talk." From Mike.

"Don't be mad at me. I was ready to do it."

Yes, Sebastian had offered, and yet, I had to wonder, did he do it because he wanted to or out of pity?

I did have some standards. Not many. But a smidgen of pride was one of them.

"I think you've all said enough." I stood, tucking my robe tight. "Go. Now. Before I call the cops." When Sebastian went to close the lid on the pizza, I did add one more thing. "Leave the food."

I'd need it.

Mike Interlude

Brenda asked them firmly to go. And yet he saw the hint of vulnerability in her.

Mike could see Dale wanted to argue and stay, Sebastian too, but he shook his head.

"I think we should go."

"But—"

"It's been a momentous day. And I think Brenda could use some rest. We all could." Mike spoke firmly and did his best to ignore Brenda's trembling lower lip.

If they stayed, someone would claim her. He could state that for a fact, but before that happened, they needed to ensure they did it for the right reasons. It was only fair to Brenda.

They left her apartment, not speaking until they hit the street.

Dale started. "We can't leave her alone. Between the collective and whatever is possessing people, she's in danger."

"We can't exactly force her to accept our company, though." Mike stared up at her window. "She thinks we're rejecting her."

"That's nuts," Dale exclaimed. "Is she blind? Can't she see how much we like her?"

"No, what she sees are three guys trying to

get in her pants because we're all vying for her attention."

"I don't see why I'm getting roped into this. I meant what I said upstairs. I'll claim her."

"No, you won't."

"Why not?"

"Because…" Dale paused. "I want to claim her, too."

"As do I," Mike muttered.

"We can't all have her." Dale's eyes sparked with jealousy.

"And therein lies the problem."

"Not a problem if we share." Sebastian shrugged as they looked at him. "Listen, we obviously like this girl. All of us. So we can either wreck a great friendship and fight over that fact, or give in to what fate obviously wants from us and claim her."

"Share her for life?" Dale said it thoughtfully. "I guess if I had to do that with anyone it would be you guys."

"And there are the tax breaks," Sebastian teased.

"There are many positives to it, with the biggest negative being dealing with our jealousy. But there's one thing we haven't really discussed. What does Brenda want?"

As one, they stared upwards and might have gone pounding back upstairs to address the issue if Dale's phone hadn't rung.

"It's Pete." And it wasn't good news.

They left Sebastian behind to guard Brenda, outside with him promising not to go inside unless there was danger. He'd spend the night on her fire escape until one of them relieved him.

Mike went along with Dale for the briefing by Pete.

The news proved alarming.

Pacing the large living room in Anthony's house, Pete filled them in. "We've identified the source of the infection."

"Back up a second," Mike asked. "Infection? Is that what they're calling the possession now?"

"Yes. We've only confirmed it in a few of the cases so far, but the evidence is mounting. All those who began to act strangely, the firemen and police, came into contact with the Peabodys. More specifically, their house. They were the first responders on the scene when Mr. Peabody was arrested."

"All of them?" Dale couldn't help but ask in a tone most startled.

"Not all, but enough to form a pattern."

"You'd better not be saying that house is contagious," Mike remarked.

"We don't think it's contagious in the usual sense. Not from host to host at any rate. We believe the only way they can become infected is if they come in close contact with the house."

"But you say not everyone is affected."

"No, and yet all the cases we've encountered have the same ground zero so far."

Dale rubbed his jaw. "Say we believe the house is somehow possessing people. How does that explain the librarian? I highly doubt she does house calls."

"The librarian is one Ethel Thorpe, and she resides at 997—"

Mike interrupted to finished. "Cloven Hoof Lane."

"She's their fucking neighbor?" Dale scrubbed his face. "This is turning into a clusterfuck."

How much of Dale's agitation stemmed from the situation or the fact that they knew Brenda had been inside that house?

Did she carry a spore inside her, a ticking time bomb?

"Has anyone checked on the other neighbors around?" Dale asked.

Pete pivoted from his pacing to face them. "TDCM has dispatched a containment crew. All residents in a two-block radius are being tested as we speak."

"So, what do we do next?"

"Nothing."

"What do you mean nothing?" Dale barked. "Something in that house is fucking with people." Possibly fucking with Brenda. She'd visited but shown no signs of possession.

Yet.

"We can't do anything." Pete shrugged. "We've been kicked off the case. We have no official capacity to get involved."

Dale looked at the vampire sitting off to the side. "Don't you have anything to say?"

At this point, Anthony, who'd remained silent to this point, nursing a brandy, spoke. "Our kind has chosen to abstain from this unfortunate situation, which means I can't advise you in regards to the current circumstances. But as an observer, I find it curious that human authorities haven't returned to the Peabody house. Not even to check on the family."

"That is surprising," Dale said slowly. "And really, peeking in on them would be the right thing to do. But the police need to have just cause to go in."

"Indeed they do," said the vampire lawyer. "I recently tried a case where the defense argued that a 911 call wasn't sufficient grounds for law enforcement to enter his client's home. They lost."

The hint was clear.

Via a burner phone bought in a corner store, Dale placed a call.

Chapter Fourteen

I woke up alone, and yet my apartment had company.

And since it wasn't one of my three wolves, I didn't feel a need to be nice about it.

"What are you doing in my place?" I asked the redhead sitting comfortably in my kitchen sipping from a Starbucks cup.

Lucky for her, she'd brought two.

"Your Lycan friends couldn't stick around and asked if I could do them a favor."

They'd sent the witch to watch over me? Ah. So sweet. Sweeter if they'd done it in person. "They sent you to babysit me?" My nose wrinkled.

"Actually, they sent me to ensure you weren't infected."

"Don't tell me they have STDs." Hold on, we hadn't engaged in penis sex yet, but I'd let Sebastian lick me. Could I get an STD from spit? I thought Lycans didn't carry disease.

"I have no idea about any sexually transmitted diseases they carry," Willow said, her nose wrinkling. "I was speaking of the infection that caused the librarian to act out."

"Am I going to turn into a psycho bitch, too?" That would suck. My life was finally starting to turn around.

"You're clean."

"Good." And kind of disappointing. It would have made interesting conversation. "So what's the plan for today?"

"I have to go to work." Willow stood. "Being a witch doesn't pay the bills."

"Work?" Ack. I looked at the time and cringed. I'd be late. Again.

But our boss knew better than to harass me about it. The last time he did, I burst into tears and told him I felt attacked because I was a woman and on my period and… I went on for a while until he turned tomato-red and ushered me from his office.

This time, he didn't even bother to say anything when I sauntered in over an hour late.

And then I took my time eating the donuts I'd grabbed on my way.

Time dragged by. Probably because I didn't work much. The mood just wasn't conducive to anything constructive today. What I was in the mood for involved two or three of the guys interested in me enough to make up their mind.

"Is it really so much to ask for?" I asked the plant sitting on my desk. "I mean, sure I could be greedy and demand all three of them claim me, but hell, I'd settle for just one person to love." Someone I could wake up beside every morning and not because I'd tied them to the bed.

"Brenda!"

Francis, the office gopher—wearing his lime-green pants and smartly tied cravat—came sauntering into the secretarial pen. The desks around me sat mostly empty, as the others had gone to lunch. I, on the other hand, saved money and brought leftover pizza. While I chewed, I took that time to speak to my cactus. It never judged me, even though I'd killed seven of its ancestors.

"What is it, Francis?" I asked, tucking the empty box away lest he comment about my appetite. The last time he'd made a remark about the amount of food I consumed we got pulled in front of HR, and I had to apologize for making a rude gesture with my mouth and hand describing Francis's favorite meal. It didn't go over well, and I spent eight hours on a Saturday undergoing sensitivity training.

It should be noted that I didn't disagree with eating sausage; I loved it. But, apparently, Francis was a vegetarian. Which made me wonder, if he didn't eat meat, did he still fuck it?

"You've been looking into that Peabody case, haven't you?" he said, stopping in front of my desk.

"Was. Nothing to find. Hubby is crazier than a meth head high on crack." And I'd promised Chloe I wouldn't go back to talk to his wife.

Then again, even if there was something to tell, I wouldn't tell Francis. He was human. So was I, but maybe I'd have a DNA test done to be sure. Wouldn't it be cool if my blood contained a little something special?

"Are you sure there's nothing? Because I heard through the police scanner that the cops were called out to their place last night."

"Really, why?" Had Mrs. Peabody gone nutso, too? Did she start flying around her yard? Trying to eat the neighborhood kids?

"Reports of screaming last night, and some God-awful smell coming from the house."

"Smell? As in someone burnt the pot roast? Septic tank is full?"

"A rotting smell," Francis confided.

My eyes widened. "Is Mrs. Peabody dead?" And more importantly, was I the last person to see her alive? If yes, that would make me a prime suspect. I wondered if I'd get a cute cop questioning me.

Bad Brenda. I should be thinking about alibis.

Francis shrugged. "No idea if anyone is dead. I haven't heard about them finding any bodies. But I hear the school informed the cop on the case that the children haven't been seen since Peabody was arrested."

"That can't be right." I almost said Mrs. Peabody had told me otherwise, but then I realized that I might be screwing myself if it did turn into a murder case. Francis would totally hang me out to dry.

"Who knows what they'll find, but I thought you should know."

He thought right. The problem was, I hungered for more than a juicy tidbit of gossip.

Seriously, I must have been a cat in another life because I was curious. I needed to go back to the house.

But Dale and the others had said to stay away. The guys had also abandoned me when the

C word came up. For once, it didn't rhyme with punt.

"Are the police still at the house?" I asked as I opened my bottom drawer to yank out my purse. It barely fit because of its bulging sides.

"They've been there for hours."

I still had about twenty minutes left on my lunch. Longer, if I faked sick.

A tiny voice reminded me that I'd promised Chloe I wouldn't go back to the Peabody place. But that was before shit had hit the fan. Besides, if the cops were already there, then how much trouble could I really get into?

On an even more positive note, cops meant handcuffs. Maybe even some frisking. I reapplied my lipstick before heading out.

Unlike my first excursion to suburbia, this time, the house seemed much shabbier. I didn't know how I'd missed the state of disrepair the last time I visited. The lawn was half dead, the weeds thrusting up from the yellow grass. The branches on the bushes were bare of leaves. The whole place had a sad air of neglect.

On a more positive note, a cop car was parked out front, along with an unmarked sedan.

Fantastic. Here was to hoping I'd not gotten the married and on a donut diet version.

I could, though, handle a girl cop. After all, she'd have handcuffs and a gun. At this point, abandoned by three guys, my bruised ego could use a stroke. Even a feminine one.

Lowering the visor to use the mirror, I did a teeth check—no pizza caught in the gaps—a breath check—better pop a mint—boob check—adjusted the girls for maximum cleavage—and then ran my fingers through my hair to give it a slightly rolled-out-of-bed look.

Opening the truck door, I leaped out and hit the pavement in my flats. I'd opted for my practical Mary Janes today just in case I had to run from a poltergeist. As I adventured, I learned. I'd also worn a skirt again in case I visited another library.

Once more, I had my handy satchel over my shoulder, opting for a multi-purpose crowbar—good for prying shit and whacking the possessed—a vial of holy water, gathered on my way to work, and a silver dagger bought off the guy on the corner. The gun was tucked in the glove box because it made my purse too heavy. At least it was nearby.

As a final protective talisman, I also wore a cross around my neck. Sure, Anthony might have told Chloe that religion didn't bother his kind, but hello, he was a vampire. What else would he tell her?

I preferred to not take any chances.

Heading up the sidewalk, determined to get inside, I'd almost made it to the front door when it opened.

And out walked Dale.

In a uniform.

A police uniform, I might add.

"You're a cop?" The incredulity in my tone was at odds with the sudden wetness in my panties.

"What are you doing here?" he asked,

grabbing me by the arm and tugging me down the walkway.

"I heard there was something going on, so I came to see."

"You shouldn't be here. You're supposed to be at work."

"I was. But then I heard about the Peabody house. What's going on?" I asked as a forensic van pulled up.

"Nothing. Go back to work."

I dug in my heels. "I am not going anywhere until you tell me what's happening."

"Nothing is happening. We had a report, and we're checking it out."

"Did you find any bodies?"

Before Dale could reply, another familiar voice called out, "What's she doing here?"

Stepping out of the forensics van was none other than Sebastian.

"You both work for the police department? How did I not know this?"

"Because we didn't tell you, and it never came up."

They did it on purpose to hide it. "I would have clued in if I'd seen you in uniform."

"Most of the time, I'm assigned plain clothes duties, but I was supposed to testify today, so I wore my uniform, only I got called to the ah...um..."

"Crime scene. You can say it."

He glared. "Get in your truck, Brenda."

"You can't order me around. I'm a citizen, and I have rights."

"Very well, you want to play by the rules." He spun me around and grabbed my wrists. The day seemed brighter. "You have the right to remain silent." He began to recite my Miranda rights as he handcuffed me.

Me? A girl he'd made out with.

He then proceeded to tuck me into the back of his car and shut the door. *Did you know there're no handles on the inside?* I couldn't get out. But I could hear.

Sebastian argued with him. "What are you doing?"

"Keeping her out of trouble."

"You can't leave her in your car all day," Sebastian hissed.

"She'd probably get into less trouble if I did," Dale snapped.

"Just get her to leave."

"What makes you think she won't just come back?"

When they both turned to stare at me, I smiled. I would have waved, but even I couldn't contort enough to get those hands up from behind my back. Which reminded me, why were they still behind my back?

With a little wiggle and effort, I managed to tuck my butt, then my legs through the loop of my arms. The boys were still arguing and didn't notice my fabulous dexterity.

Even through the closed window, I heard Dale sigh. "I'll take care of this. If anyone asks, tell them I went to get coffee. I'll be back as soon as I can."

He settled himself behind the wheel, and I leaned forward, not touching the mesh between our seats. Who knew what had licked it? "You can't arrest me. I haven't done anything wrong."

"You've done plenty of things wrong, but we're not going to the station."

Nor were we apparently going to my place. Instead, we went to his house, and when I refused to get out of the car, he leaned in and dragged me out then tossed me over a brawny shoulder, where I protested for the sake of it.

Despite his high-handed manner, the whole situation was kind of hot, especially since his hand rested on my bare thigh, holding me in place.

As soon as we entered the house, his hand slid higher, cupping an ass cheek.

"You are the most vexing woman I've ever met, kitten."

"Does that mean you're going to spank me?" I asked. I couldn't help a shiver of excitement.

"I should." He caressed my cheek. "But I doubt you'd learn a lesson. More than likely, you'd do it on purpose to get in trouble again."

How well he already knew me.

He carried me up the stairs, my big, strong man bringing me to his bed, and me still in handcuffs.

Oh, the possibilities.

He tossed me on his mattress, and I bounced with a squeal. He quickly covered my body with his, his hands pulling my wrists over my head, and I caught my breath.

"What now, Scooby?"

Now was time for a kiss. His mouth swooped onto mine, claiming it in a torrid embrace that slapped all my nerve endings awake.

His tongue lashed mine, sliding and teasing, sucking it even. I wished I could touch him, but he had my hands secured, which in itself was very hot.

His body pressed heavily against mine, and my hips undulated against him.

"I can't wait to feel you inside me," I breathed against his ear before nibbling it.

"I wish we had time for that. But I have to go. And I can't return smelling of sex."

Go? "Oh, hell no, Scooby. You can't leave me hanging. Or would you prefer to go back to work knowing I'm pleasuring myself?"

That drew a growl from him, and another torrid kiss. It also brought his hand skimming up my thigh, brushing against the damp crotch of my panties. He pushed them out of his way, and I cried out as he ran his finger along my wet slit.

"Maybe I can spare a minute to please you," he murmured against my mouth.

A minute? Maybe seconds. I was already on fire for him.

The stroke of his fingers against my sex only made it hotter. My hips thrust against his hand as he dipped a finger in and out, then two fingers.

He pushed and pulled, stretching me, his thumb teasing my clit, driving my pleasure. Heightening my need.

"Please. I need more," I cried as I sat on the brink of ecstasy.

He tore his mouth from mine, and for a moment, I know he meant to put it somewhere else. He wasn't going to leave me hanging.

But then his fucking phone rang.

And he withdrew his fingers from me.

He left the room with a softly muttered, "Sorry, kitten. I gotta go. I'll be back as soon as I can."

"No. Don't you fucking dare leave me." I tried to roll off the bed, only to discover that not only was I still handcuffed, he'd also tethered me once again to his headboard.

"You fucking bastard, come back here and let me go."

Come back here and make me come.

What kind of cruelty involved getting a girl so horny she thought she'd die then leaving?

In that moment, I could totally see the case for neutering dogs.

Once I get loose...

Watch out.

Which reminded me, I'd worn my special charm bracelet today. I should add it wasn't the four leaf clover on it that made it lucky.

In between cutesy charms, like the frog prince and a tiny tiara, it held a few different cuff keys. Chloe had bought it for me after the Jason incident. Douchetard left me handcuffed to the bed. Gagged, I might add.

Totally mean, especially since I hadn't intended to laugh at his cock. But when it disappeared because of the cold draft from the fan in my room...

I popped free and rubbed my wrists. I held off on rubbing any other parts. I had two choices at the moment. I could get my ass back to the Peabody house. Or I could stick around and explore the place.

Guess what I chose?

Dale Interlude

So many emotions gripped Dale.

Guilt because he'd left Brenda. Left her not just tied and defenseless but also aroused.

So very, very aroused and wet.

Having lately been the recipient of blue balls, he could well imagine her annoyance at that cruel trick.

However, what choice did he have? If he had sex with her, knowing he and his friends still hadn't made a decision, what kind of rift would he cause?

Best to leave when sanity in the form of a text message slapped him, reminding him to grab six coffees and some donuts. Was that Sebastian's subtle way of ensuring Dale didn't do something he shouldn't but wanted?

He wished he didn't have to leave Brenda tied up. But she'd proven herself too reckless to leave alone.

Dale didn't leave her completely unprotected, though. He called in some favors and had two pack members watching the house. If she managed to free herself from cuffs—which Dale didn't put past her—and left, they had orders to let him know and follow.

Dale wasn't about to give anyone orders to lay hands on her because if they accidentally harmed her, he'd have to kill them.

No one is allowed to touch her but me. And Mike. And Sebastian.

Funny how more and more the thought of them sharing Brenda didn't bother him. He didn't want to rip off their faces and stomp on their heads.

Could a foursome work?

Returning to the Peabody house, loaded with coffee and pastries, and with a text message from the guys watching his house informing him that, "Some hillbilly chick is cursing up a storm in your place," he tried to focus on the case at hand.

While Anthony had slyly suggested them calling in a fake report to give themselves entry into the house, it proved quickly apparent, once dispatch finally got its thumb out of its ass, that something very wrong had happened at the Peabody house. Dale could smell, it, the thick aroma of decay and earth. Feel it in the way the air grew still and heavy in and around the house.

Sense it with the hackles rising all over his body.

He could see why Peabody wanted to burn it down. Hell, give him a match, and he'd finish the job.

But his commanding officer might not like that.

How would the report read?

It was evil. I torched it.

Clang, the sound of the bars slamming shut

behind him.

Probably best he refrained.

Knowing about the infection causing possession, Dale and those of the crypto community working at the police department had to carefully ensure that no humans were sent out to the house. It took a bit of figuring it out, but the TDCM scientists discovered why some showed signs of infection and others didn't.

At first, the collective tried to hide the news, but it leaked out. Essentially, shifters were immune to possession, as were pure-blooded elves and most higher castes in the cryptozoid world. Even some humans were immune if they had significant amounts of magic in their system. However, magic imbued humans, even non-practicing ones, weren't entirely safe because whatever happened to the infected bodies made them hungry for anyone with an ounce of magic in their blood.

Since no humans could be sent to the Peabody house, it caused a delay on the 911 reply, as the pack had to ensure all other working cops on shift were occupied elsewhere.

There was much howling that night, and many, many calls to 911.

It took until the morning shift before Dale and his partner, Willy—a bear shifter who mostly spoke in grunts—got dispatched to the call for 999 Cloven Hoof Lane. Arriving just past 8 a.m., and totally finding cause to kick in the door when no one answered, the sight inside meant they'd been here ever since.

Hours of looking, though, hadn't turned up shit other than a case of the heebie-jeebies.

Inside the house, everything looked old and gray. As if the color and life had been sucked out of every inch.

The parquet floors heaved and buckled, damp with moisture and mildew. The walls bore heavy stains and peeling paper while parts of the ceiling had collapsed, raining plaster and dull pink insulation.

Everywhere Dale looked, he saw signs of a house severely neglected, and yet he'd read the reports when they arrested Peabody just over a week ago.

None of them spoke of a house in major need of renovation.

They did mention the wife, Mrs. Peabody, looking calmer than you'd expect after calling the cops and fire department for aid.

She'd stood with her arms around the two children while they led her husband away. The next day, she'd come to the station to give her statement, a mousy woman with nondescript kids.

A woman not seen since, except by Brenda.

He had to wonder why Brenda would have eaten anything in this dump. What person in their right mind would have even entered?

And where were Mrs. Peabody and the kids?

Alfred, that possessed shell of a man, remained locked up at the asylum. The grand Whizziar and a contingent of wizards had been to visit and managed to eject the thing possessing him. To no avail. Even with the parasitic force gone, nothing remained of the man. Whatever had attached itself to Peabody's mind and soul had eaten whatever personality he had. According to Mike, Peabody sat in an almost comatose state, wearing a bib to catch the drool, unresponsive to anything, even the color red.

Apparently, the wizards had seen some success with other cases, some of the cops and firemen cleansed, but those caught feasting seemed to be more firmly entrenched with the parasitic infection the more blood they imbibed.

Feeding made them gain strength, and their attacks were no longer just witches. Ordinary people with even a smidgen of talent were victims.

The collective seemed to think they'd contained the problem by quarantining those who came in contact with the house, but Dale had to wonder. They'd only cloistered those they knew about. Were there others walking around infected?

Handing out coffee, he caught snippets of what they'd found or, more specifically, not found. Still no sign of any bodies.

Nor any signs of life.

Food rotted in the sink. Dirty dishes were on the table. Everything in the fridge was moldy and gross.

That was just what they could see on the surface.

The wizards, including the pompous Morfeus, muttered excitedly amongst themselves and, par for the course, didn't share with those they considered lesser beings.

Only Willow, her red hair a vibrant contrast in the house, seemed amenable to talking. She left the wizards and came to him, her eyes rolling.

"What's up?" Dale asked, handing her the coffee meant for Sebastian.

"These idiots can't agree on anything."

"Because they're idiots." Wizards might go to a prestigious magical university, but as with many scholars, they let it go to their heads.

"This place is wrong."

"Wrong how?"

She hugged herself. "I can't explain it except that it feels wrong."

"So I'm not alone in wanting to light a match?"

Her lips quirked. "Match. Blowtorch. Whatever happened here is still ongoing."

"Are we safe?"

She frowned. "I hope so. But whatever is in this house keeps trying to get past my defenses." She touched an amulet hanging from her neck.

"Can you be infected?"

Her lips twisted. "I guess we'll find out. I am, after all, mostly human, as his grand assholeness keeps reminding me."

"What's causing the infection?" he asked.

"Demons."

He frowned. "Are you sure?" Couldn't it be a moldy spore? Even some new type of avian flu?

"I can't be sure of anything, but the pattern fits what I've been able to discover."

"There's a record of this happening before?"

She nodded. "I found a few references to it, enough to make me believe it's happening again. See, demons exist on another dimension, one that rarely aligns with our own. When it does, most of them cannot exist on our plane, not unless they possess someone first. And even then, they can't hold on to that possession unless they feed on blood."

"Witch blood."

"Witch. Half-breed elf. Pure-blood elves are like poison to them, and humans without any magic are just empty nutrition."

"What happens if they drink enough magical blood?"

"They evolve. Their host creature can then transform, much like a Lycan can, swapping into their demon form without coming to harm."

"I thought demons couldn't exist in our world without some ritual."

She shrugged. "This is all new to me, too, and I only accidentally learned by the snippets I've overheard. Needless to say, the wizards are nervous and guarding themselves carefully."

"Would a person know if they were possessed?"

"Maybe, but I doubt the demon possessing would let you tell."

"This doesn't sound good for the family," Dale remarked.

"I am fairly certain that if they're not dead, then they are beyond saving, if that's what you're asking."

"Are you sure Lycans can't catch it?" He'd

hate to turn into a raving lunatic like Peabody or end up like meat slurry.

"I'm not sure of anything anymore. I've never encountered or heard of anything like this." She leaned closer. "And while the twat waffles with their fancy words won't admit it, they've never seen the likes of it either."

"So how do we know their information is accurate?"

Her shoulders lifted and fell. "We don't, which is why I'm hoping the spell in this amulet, and my great-great-grandmother's elven blood, will make me immune to whatever is happening."

Dale went to lean against a wall in the house, felt it ripple, and moved away. "I'm surprised to see you still working with the wizards. I'd have thought Morfeus would have bumped you off by now."

Her lips curved into a smile. "They threatened to, and then I told them if they didn't keep me in the loop, I'd make sure the world knew about their snotty college and everyone who's ever graduated from it."

"And you're still alive?"

Her grin widened. "I also told them if I died, the information would release within minutes of my passing, so they were better off tolerating a hearth witch. It might have helped that I asked Morfeus if he was threatened by me."

"I'll bet he liked that." Dale snorted.

"The man is a pompous fool enamored with himself. But in spite of that, he is powerful."

"Powerful enough to contain what's

happening here?"

Again, she shrugged. "You'd better hope he can."

Ominous words that followed Dale back to the station, where he filed his report, which, in a nutshell, amounted to: found nothing.

He had Mike grab him at the station rather than wait for Sebastian to snare a ride. Going back to the Peabodys' place, he hopped into Brenda's truck, intending to drive it back to his house, only the damned thing wouldn't start. Just a clicking sound every time he turned the key.

"Sounds like the starter's gone," Mike remarked when Dale jumped out.

"No shit. We'll have to get it towed."

"Towed where? I hear you left Brenda at our place."

"I did."

"We have to make a decision," Mike remarked.

"I know."

He'd also have to beg for forgiveness because he doubted Brenda would be too happy about the way he left her.

Which was why, when they got back, they initially left her tied as they entered the bedroom, all three of them, ready to face the future.

And her wrath.

Chapter Fifteen

I had a grand time exploring their house. Digging through their drawers. Discovering Sebastian's secret porn stash. Mike's Reese's Pieces cups hidden inside a hollow book. As for Dale, he had bath salts that I quite enjoyed.

When I heard them pulling into the driveway, I'd put myself back to bed, in the handcuffs.

I had a glare—and a sexy pose—ready for them when they walked through the door.

"About time you came back," I snapped. "What if I had to pee?"

"Do you?" Sebastian asked, reaching for me.

"No. But that's not the point. You can't just handcuff me to a bed anytime you want."

"Why not?" Dale tossed me a male grin that included a onceover. "You look good all tied up, if you ask me."

"Flattery won't work on me, Scooby, not after what you did."

"Don't you mean *didn't* do?"

Where did this playful Dale come from? And damn him for being so hot.

"What Dale means to say is that he's truly

sorry for restraining you." Sebastian and his flowery words.

"No, he's not," said Mike. "And I would have done the same thing. Vixen here doesn't know how to stay out of trouble."

"You might have a point," I admitted. "But I feel I should add that the trouble I get into is my business and not yours."

"That's where you're wrong. What if we made it our business?"

"What's this *we* stuff? Weren't you guys the ones spouting off about me choosing?" The same ones who'd taken off last night, leaving me alone.

If they cared so much, wouldn't at least one of them have stayed?

"What if you didn't have to choose?" Dale said slowly.

"Are you saying what I think you're saying, or am I hallucinating some hidden dirty meaning because it's what I want and not what you want?"

"As usual, you talk too much," Dale stated.

I might have taken more offense; however, the men approached the bed, one on each side, Dale at the foot.

"What are you doing?" I licked my lips, and I knew I should be scared. So scared, especially considering these three men had shown nothing but disdain for me—and attraction. But did the one trump the other?

I didn't see contempt in their gazes anymore. I didn't see anger or dislike.

On the contrary, their eyes glowed, and as a girl who enjoyed a good meal, I recognized their expression.

Hunger.

Hunger for me.

But what kind of hunger? Did these men who could turn into wolves plan to eat me to solve their problem?

I should be so lucky.

"Is this going to hurt?"

"What if we promise to make it hurt so good?" Sebastian winked a moment before he took off his shirt.

I gaped.

Possibly drooled. I definitely wasn't thinking straight.

"Our guest is under the impression we don't find her attractive," Dale stated.

"Is she fucking blind?" Mike snapped.

My gaze bobbed over to where he stood on my left, and I couldn't help a squeeze of my va-jay-jay because he stood there shirtless, his upper body huge and muscled while his jeans... The top button was undone, and I could see the fine vee leading down...

Oh, my.

Definite bulge in the groin area.

Mike was also on board?

I didn't expect all three men, yes *three*, to shed their clothes and blind me with their magnificent bodies.

"I must have died."

I didn't realize I'd spoken out loud until Dale chuckled. "Not yet, but you'll feel like you have and gone to Heaven by the time we're done with you."

Had a woman ever heard more promising words?

I didn't understand their change of heart, but I couldn't deny my excitement. Call me a slut, but I'd gone from angry at them to scared to highly aroused.

They were finally acting the way I expected. The way I wanted.

If this is a dream, don't let me wake.

Especially not before the good parts.

With three sets of hands, my clothes didn't stand a chance. So long, suckers!

Exposed, it didn't take long before three mouths suddenly landed on my body, each man choosing a spot and caressing my bare skin with their lips.

Under their expert caresses, my body ignited, and a gasp parted my lips. My blood heated, and my sex got wet, so very, very wet with honey. Without a touch, my nipples tightened, attention whores looking for some action.

But the men seemed intent on simply tasting my skin. Brushing their lips over my sensitized flesh. Making me shiver and moan and undulate.

This wasn't my first multi-partner rodeo. I'd done my share of experimenting, but usually, it evolved into two guys doing each other while I watched and wondered if it was rude to leave.

Not a problem with these fellows. Their focus was 100 percent on little ol' me. And I loved it.

A good thing they'd tied me up because I would have thrown myself on them, wanton slut looking for some action.

Even tied up, I wasn't quiet about the fact that I wanted them. Craved them. I moaned and begged.

No shame.

None at all.

And they chuckled, they nibbled, they sipped at my flesh, igniting it.

A sharp cry left me as finally one of them latched on to an erect peak, his hot mouth tugging, sucking, and pulling.

It drove me wild, and my hips arched, only to get slammed back down.

"You're not going anywhere yet, kitten. Not until we're done."

Promising words, but even more promising were the butterfly kisses moving up the inside of my thigh, the soft caresses teasing my flesh while another mouth blew on my sex.

Maddening. Torturous.

I might have harangued them for their cruelty, except I had a tongue in my mouth.

Mmm. Finally, one of them kissed me, latched his mouth to mine, and let me taste him. I did more than that. I sucked at his tongue, the only thing I could touch, and so I lavished all my attention on it.

Desire built inside me, each stroke, each caress making me taut with expectation. All of me sensitized and aroused on the very edge of ultimate pleasure.

And then the fuckers withdrew. I wasn't nice about it.

"Don't you dare fucking stop."

"Don't worry, kitten, we're not done."

"It ain't over until she screams," Mike said, the words ominous, but his lips on mine showed erotic intent.

I felt something slap me, two somethings, three. Three cocks, all for me?

I wished I could touch them, wrap my hands around their shafts and tug them. Guide them into my throbbing flesh.

Some people thought ultimate pleasure could only come with emotional commitment. I dared them to change spots with me right now and not cream themselves with pleasure.

Mike withdrew his mouth, and I mewled in disappointment and then sighed with delight because, through my heavy eyelids, I saw him stroking a very, and I mean very, thick cock.

But my attention was quickly drawn when a mouth decided in that moment to latch itself onto my sex.

"Fuck me."

Yeah, I screamed a very unladylike thing, but they didn't seem to mind, at least the mouth on my pussy didn't, given it sucked at my tender lips, tongued my slit, but when he decided to start flicking against my clit?

I came.

Came hard.

Furious.

And screaming.

They weren't done with me yet.

Panting from excitement, the muscles in my channel spasming, my open mouth acted as an invitation. My lips were nudged apart to make room for a cock.

About fucking time. I sucked, head bobbing, wishing I had my hands, but then didn't care as a dick covered in latex—good boy—made its way into my sex.

Yes!

The thick shaft pushed into me, stretching my still quivering muscles. I couldn't help but clench tighter, and that brought a groaned, "Baby, you're going to kill me."

Sebastian. My what a nice dick he had. It pushed deeper into me, his curved prick not stopping until it hit my sweet spot. Then he began a thrusting dance of pull out, push in, a seesawing that started out slow but picked up speed. Hitting my G-spot. Filling me up.

Oh, fuck me. It felt so good.

I managed to moan my appreciation around the cock in my mouth, the humming sound making Mike dig his fingers into my hair as he strained not to come.

Yeah. No, he was coming whether he wanted to or not.

I sucked harder, took him deeper, heard him moaning and almost bit him as lips latched onto my nipple, biting the tip.

Mike didn't mind the grazing of my teeth on his cock. I heard him hiss, "Yesss."

The cock thrusting into me quickened in

pace, each stroke slamming into my body with fleshy smacks. It was making my body taut again, building that pleasure inside.

Hands grasped my ass and tilted me, allowing his cock to sink even deeper, banging hard against my sweet spot.

So hard.

So good.

Again and again.

I came again, my whole body jerking as pleasure rolled through me.

And still, they weren't done.

Mouth full of cock, a cock throbbing hard, I only vaguely noticed when my arms were freed, putting me at the mercy of hands that flipped me onto my stomach then slid me atop a hard body. Dale's body.

His lips caught mine as the hands continued to maneuver me into place, pulling on me until I was poised above his cock.

Then pushing me down on it.

I'd just come, but there was still something incredibly erotic and exciting about the way they were moving me, rocking me on Dale's hard prick.

And then I felt the tickle at my ass.

I think they're going to go for a double.

I'd heard of it but never tried it.

No time like the present.

Since I was kissing Dale, it took a moment for me to feel the tap on my shoulder. I turned to look sideways and found Mike's big cock back against my lips. Half seated, I sucked on him as Dale penetrated me. As for Sebastian, the cold dribble between my cheeks was followed by the finger rubbing at my rosette.

Despite having done this a few times before, I couldn't help but tense as a finger probed my tight hole.

To distract me, the cock in my mouth began its own in-and-out cadence, drawing my attention, while the hands on my waist swirled and pushed me down harder on the prick impaling me.

The finger in my ass eased in deeper, and it felt so incredibly strange, but not bad.

The cock in my pussy stroked me harder, making me ignore the finger sliding in and out with ease in my ass. Forgotten until a second digit shoved its way in.

The tightness of my rosette made me squirm as he stretched me, but it wasn't long before my pleasure overcame my trepidation and I was riding those fingers as hard as the cock.

I bounced and rocked, having a grand ol' time until the fingers pulled out and a cock pushed its way in.

Everything froze for a moment. Maybe because I squeaked.

Fingers were one thing, but a big fat cock…

It took me a moment to adjust, and Sebastian whispered, "Relax, baby. I promise you'll like this."

He reached under me, my body currently joined with Dale's, and found my clit. He pinched it, and I cried out around the cock in my mouth. And he kept pinching and rubbing as he rode me, his motion driving us all, his cadence setting the pace.

In and out. I couldn't have said where my body began and ended, where my pleasure started or finished. All I knew was my body began tensing for a third time.

A third fucking orgasm.

How?

God.

I am pretty sure I screamed when it hit, the intensity just too much. I might have clamped down on all the dicks penetrating me. Mike came, pulling his dick free instead of filling my mouth.

Because of the condoms, I didn't feel the hot cream of the other two coming, but I felt the connection. A jolt of awareness. Joining. Felt it to the very depth of my being.

And then I passed out.

Mike Interlude

He wanted to smile.

Which, in turn, made Mike want to slap himself. Since that would look insane, he rolled off the bed instead and stalked off.

He should have known Dale would follow.

"What's wrong?"

"We shouldn't have done that," Mike growled.

"She was willing."

"I know she was willing, but we shouldn't have taken advantage. Not all three of us like that. We didn't really give her much choice."

"She didn't say no."

"She never exactly had a chance to say yes either," Mike grumbled. He wasn't really sure what was wrong with him.

He'd just had mind-blowing oral. As in, holy fuck, I almost shot a load in her mouth oral. And now, he was thinking the unthinkable. Thinking of claiming her with his three best friends, which, in turn, caused a moment of panic.

"It will be okay," Dale said. "I think we're all freaking out a bit. I know I am. This wasn't how I expected things to turn out."

"What happens now?" Mike asked.

"Now, we sleep. Maybe fuck some more after a shower when we wake up."

Except that plan never came to pass.

Duty meant they had to leave in the middle of the night. The pack called, and they had to answer.

Not usually the sentimental type, Mike couldn't resist stroking the blonde strands from her face. Something in him tightened when she smiled in her sleep.

He rubbed his chest.

I'll have to get that checked out.

Or maybe it was time to admit that Brenda wasn't a passing fancy. She was here to stay. And after what had happened last night, he wouldn't be alone.

They were, however, leaving her alone.

"Should we be abandoning her like this?" Mike asked, looking upstairs. Brenda still slept. Deeply. A smile on her lips.

"We don't have a choice. The pack called a meeting to talk about the Peabody house issue."

"You mean the ongoing threat of it. Do we all have to go? It's dangerous for her to be alone." Brenda had a way of finding trouble.

"Dangerous only if she goes wandering. Which she won't. I've got some boys in place to keep an eye on her. And, besides, how is she going to get anywhere? Her truck is still outside Peabody's place, and I've got her wallet." Dale held up her purse. "Chances are, we'll be back before she wakes. But if it makes you feel better, leave her a note."

A note. Right. What exactly should he say? *Thanks for the mind-blowing night. I think I'm falling in love.*

Ack. Shoot me, I'm getting sappy.

Mike stuck to something simple rather than make an ass of himself.

Turned out he should have gotten Sebastian to write it or tied her back to the bed.

Chapter Sixteen

I woke up alone. Naked yet covered in a comforter. Body pleasantly sore. But alone.

Seriously?

Sitting up, I looked around the bedroom and noted, for the second time in as many days, its plain masculine décor from the heavy wooden furniture with its dark mahogany stain to the blue-patterned Berber carpet on the floor.

The comforter, no surprise, was more plaid, well-worn and soft. Heavy on my naked body. The guys had at least covered me before abandoning me.

Speaking of guys, where had they gone?

I clutched the fabric to my chest and wondered if they'd decided on a group endeavor to make breakfast because I could use some food right about now. A stack of pancakes smothered in butter and dripping syrup, freshly crisped bacon, the very salty kind, a glass of orange juice—you know, for some healthy vitamins—coffee to slap me awake, scrambled eggs, toast, mustn't forget the jam, and some sausage—and I didn't care what kind.

Rumble. My tummy totally agreed. All those orgasms made a girl hungry.

And not just for food. My va-jay-jay might have gotten a good workout, but it had a little quiver at the reminder of the previous night.

I am such a slut.

Fucking three best friends at once.

Talk about fun.

Especially since they made it all about me.

No wonder Chloe glowed since meeting her two guys. Did they always have sex in multiples?

And did this mean my wolves had claimed me? An inquiring girl wanted to know.

Exiting the bed, I noticed my clothes in a tidy pile with a note on top.

How sweet.

My smile turned upside down as I read it.

Had fun. Had to run. Later.

Later? What the hell did that mean?

Where did all three of them go? What was so fucking important that they couldn't at least say goodbye first? And how early did they run off? The alarm clock on the nightstand said 7:13 a.m. Barely past dawn.

Was it police business? That perhaps explained Dale and Sebastian, but I highly doubted Mike could fall back on the same excuse.

Did they expect me to hang around waiting for them? Then again, given my past history with guys, this was more likely a case of "thank you, get out."

They'd gotten their pound of flesh—and I'd gotten several poundings of flesh—and no big surprise, they vanished by morning.

Except, in this case, I was in their bed, not

mine, when they snuck out.

Even worse, I didn't have my wheels with me because they'd brought me here.

Ugh.

Getting dressed, I noticed my purse missing. I found my shoes, though, by the front door, but still no purse. What I did have was my phone, still tucked in a pocket. Good thing I had an Uber app that didn't require cash.

About ten minutes later—having devoured the leftover carton of Kentucky Fried chicken left in the fridge—my ride arrived. About to open the door to do the walk of shame to the blue Prius idling at the curb, I noticed a pair of guys getting out of a car across the road and talking to my Uber driver.

Babysitters? Or something else?

I'd not forgotten the warning that the wizards might want to fry me, or turn me into a frog. Since green wasn't my color, it occurred to me that, perhaps, I should use a different exit.

The back door led to a yard with a fence. As if that would stand in my way. A chair to boost me and over I went, landing in a tomato patch. Splat.

Cursing about the wet red spot on my pants—not a first because my periods had it out for me—I trudged through that yard and two more before I dared head back toward the street. I rebooked my Uber, and he arrived a moment later, waving his hands and ranting, probably about the fact that I'd sent him to the wrong address first.

"Oh, can it, you'll get paid," I snapped.

The driver didn't speak much English,

which was good because I wasn't in the mood to chat.

Shocking, I know, but I felt kind of let down. After the intense passion, stupid me thought it meant something. I don't know why I expected things would be different. Experience had taught me I just didn't have that captivating quality other girls did when it came to keeping guys.

Maybe I sucked at sex.

Maybe I screamed wrong when I came.

Did I fart and not notice it when all my muscles relaxed? Surely, there was a reason I couldn't keep a man.

Meemaw thought I was perfect. Why didn't anyone else?

I really wished I could call her and vent. She'd totally listen and then tell me to kick them in the balls if they didn't know what kind of treasure I was.

But Meemaw was still on her cruise and unreachable by phone.

Sigh. And I didn't want to burden Chloe with my sad tale of being a loser.

Initially, I meant to go home, get changed, and maybe make it into work—eventually. But how would I get to work? Since my truck wasn't in Dale's driveway, then that meant my baby was still at the Peabodys' place. Just to be sure, I checked my GPS tracker.

The day I'd bought Big Blue, I had her tagged before she even left the car lot.

The Uber fellow dropped me off in front of the Peabody place, and I gasped to see how much it had changed overnight.

The day, while overcast, couldn't entirely account for the dark pall hanging over the house. All the grass appeared dead now. Not a single trace of color remained on any of the foliage.

Despite being in suburbia, the silence was deafening. I strained to hear a single lawnmower or barking dog. Even the buzz of a bee or a slamming car door.

Unbroken quiet.

Very eerie. Very cool.

The front door of the house held a few crisscrossing bands of yellow police tape.

Do Not Enter.

Um, might as well hold up a neon sign screaming, *come check me out.*

Dale hadn't let me inside the day before. Stupid, overprotective jerk. My heart warmed and pitter-pattered a little faster.

Then I remembered the note they'd left me.

Later. What did that mean? Was it over? Would I see them again? I didn't want to be that desperate chick who called them asking.

Despite Big Blue sitting on the curb, waiting for my loving touch, I found myself heading toward the house.

The vacant house. Mrs. Peabody and the kids were missing. Gone according to the news app I'd read on the way over.

The police had no clues or suspects. I guess the super wizard dudes didn't want to admit ghosts or something might be getting rid of people. Or was it the house eating them? We never did find that priest.

The last time I'd visited, I'd not gotten any ominous vibes off the place. Now, however, it looked rather sad and lonely.

A poor house that had lost its family.

All it wanted was someone to live inside. Someone to fill its rooms with smiles and laughter.

That person could be me. I could love the house.

My hand turned the knob, and to my surprise, it opened. Careless of the cops to leave it unlocked.

Surely, it was a sign I should go in.

Yes, go in. There's nothing wrong with this house.

The door opened on silent hinges, and I expelled a sharp breath at what I saw inside.

What happened to the lovely home I'd visited a few days ago? Was this even the same place?

I stepped inside the decrepit interior and gaped. Where had the freshly painted walls and gleaming floors gone? This place looked like an entire generation had passed since its last update.

My fingers trailed over the wall, feeling the dampness, the dust. I stopped at the picture frame. The image within seemed familiar.

Because I'd seen it before when I'd visited with Mrs. Peabody. However, the barfing and other things had made me forget, forget that the woman in the picture looked nothing like the Mrs. Peabody I'd had coffee and cookies with.

The woman in the picture looked like the one in the file. A mother and wife married to a dowdy shoe salesman. So who then was the woman I'd met?

What happened here? Perhaps Dale was right. I swam out of my depth. A simple human girl, I should stick to what I knew.

Don't go. Stay.

I frowned. It sounded like my inner voice. Came from inside my head, but...

Who the fuck is talking to me?

And what possessed me—pun totally intended—to come inside? Did I want to become Spinerella's twin?

I turned around ready to march out, but the front door slammed shut.

A cool wind whistled past, floating strands of my hair, pimpling my flesh.

The creak of a floorboard from behind had me whirling.

The woman who'd fed me the nasty cookies stood there, the only spot of vibrant life, the red spark in her eyes bright.

"Well, hello there, Brenda. So nice of you to come and visit."

"Who are you?" I asked. "And don't say Mrs. Peabody." I jabbed my finger at the frame. "That's Mrs. Peabody."

A laugh bubbled from her, deeper than expected, rich with mirth, the kind that dragged nails down your spine and somehow made a sound. "But I am Mrs. Peabody. The new and improved version."

"You possessed her."

"How else was I to stay in this world? My body wasn't made for this space." Her nose wrinkled. "Now, it is." She stroked her hands down her body, her hands skimming the curves showcased in her hugging knit dress.

"What about the kids?"

Her lips curved into a secretive smile. "They have new owners, too. And so shall you shortly."

"No, thank you." I whirled for the door, only to have an invisible fist grab me and turn me back around.

"Leaving so soon?" Said in a taunting lilt. "Won't you stay for a while?"

"I'd rather not. I'm expected elsewhere."

"I'm afraid you won't make that meeting." She took a step toward me. "You're not going anywhere, Brenda. Not when you smell so good."

Again with the food thing.

I, Brenda Whittaker, am not a meal.

Actually, that wasn't entirely true. Wolves could dine all they liked on the Brenda buffet. Demons, no. I had to draw the line somewhere.

Grabbing the picture from the wall, I threw it at the Peabody body snatcher and ran for the door. At least, that was my plan.

But the floor abruptly crumbled, leaving me teetering on the edge, and I leaned against the wall, trying to catch my balance.

And that was when the house swallowed me.

Dale Interlude

"What do you mean she's gone?" Dale asked less than an hour later. They'd only been gone a few hours. Returning early enough, they'd hoped to still catch her in bed.

As Sebastian tripped down the stairs, he shrugged. "Bed's empty and cold. She's not upstairs."

"Or on this floor," Mike added.

"She left? Why would she do that?" Dale frowned. "Didn't you leave her a note?" he asked Mike.

"I did."

"You mean this note?" Sebastian held it up and read it. "Had fun. Had to run. Later."

Dale's brow's shot up. "Did you seriously not put anything else? Like, hey, there's coffee in the cupboard, a spare toothbrush in the bathroom? We'll see you in a few hours?"

Mike shrugged. "I condensed it."

"For a shrink, you're awfully clueless. She more than likely took off, thinking we're assholes who just used her for sex."

"Instead of being pissed at me, how about being mad at the idiots outside who didn't see her leaving?" Mike jabbed a finger in their direction.

"Oh, I intend to speak to them." With his fist. Dale had given them one simple task. Just one. Watch over Brenda. And they'd failed miserably. Worse, they had no idea where she'd gone.

"Well, this isn't how I'd planned to spend our day." Dale eyed the box of pastries and the tray of coffees they'd grabbed on their way home. Getting called in for a debriefing in the middle of the night about their role in the demon affair wasn't his idea of a good time. Especially since it took hours, as the wizards felt a need to question everyone and everything more than once.

"Don't freak out, bro." Sebastian held up his hands in a cool-it gesture. "No big deal. She probably had shit to do, so she took off. It is a work day. She could even be in her office. We'll track her down."

"At her office without any fresh clothes?" Mike mused aloud, "She'd go home first."

"Or," Dale added, "maybe she went to pick up her truck from the garage? Which one did you send it to?"

At the blank look on Sebastian's face, a sinking feeling filled Dale's stomach. "Mike, please tell me you at least thought to have it moved from the Peabodys' place?"

The ashen features on his friend's face answered that question.

"Surely, she wouldn't have returned there." Dale said it and immediately groaned.

Mike echoed it. "Of course she would because she's a moron."

"I'm sure she'd label it fearless." Sebastian

chuckled. "She certainly is a handful."

More than a handful, and oh so precious to Dale, to all of them, especially after last night.

"We're assuming she went to get it. Perhaps we're freaking out for nothing. Maybe she just went home." Sebastian tossed out a likely scenario.

"Without money?" Dale still had her purse.

"But did you think to shake down her clothes for a phone? You can pay for a lot of things, including a cab, with a simple tap these days."

"You're not helping," Dale growled.

"How about we call her phone and see if she answers?" Mike provided the voice of reason.

The phone rang and rang and rang, finally getting answered by the voicemail. *"You've reached my awesome ass, but I'm too busy to answer you right now, so leave a message, and if you're hot, I'll get back to you."*

Hanging up, Dale sighed. "Now what?"

"I'll go check her place," Sebastian offered.

Mike shook his head. "We need to start thinking instead of reacting, which means, before we run off half-cocked, why don't we call her best friend?"

But reacting felt so much better than thinking about what might have happened. It wasn't just demons and the Peabodys they had to worry about, but the collective, too. Dale and the others had fended off their queries about Brenda, but that didn't mean those bastards wouldn't act behind their backs.

Mike's idea had merit, though. Dale dialed Chloe, who answered on the second ring. "Hello."

"Have you heard from Brenda?" He skipped the pleasantries.

"Is something wrong?" Chloe's pleasant tone turned sharp with worry.

"That's what we're trying to find out. We left Brenda somewhere safe, only she managed to escape, and now we're trying to find her."

"Sounds like Brenda. Hold on. Let me find her phone with my app. It's how we keep tabs on each other in case we get kidnapped by men who want to use us for our epic bodies."

"They'd die." A claim uttered in the background on Chloe's end.

"Painfully." Another comment.

Dale could understand the sentiment. He was feeling pretty dangerous right about now.

Chloe made a noise. "Oh dear."

While he could probably guess why she said it, Dale still had to ask. "Where is she?"

"The Peabodys' house." Chloe then went on a rant. "Why does she do this to me? I told her not to go there. It's dangerous. I swear she's trying to turn me gray." Then she burst into tears.

The phone got passed to someone else.

A brusque, "Get your ass over there pronto to find her," from Pete.

"We're leaving."

No question, but they would go find her.

They piled into Mike's car, Dale taking shotgun. As his usually calm and collected bro took the corners at deadly speeds, his phone rang.

Dale answered it, despite the fact that the display showed private caller. "Lost and Found

Kennels, where we sniff crotches for free."

"Your attempts at humor are falling flat. What a surprise."

"Who is this?"

"Where is the female?"

Only one man he'd recently met had that pompous tone. "Why are you looking for her?" Because if the grand Whizziar searched for Brenda, it didn't bode well.

"The why isn't important. Do you have her in your custody? Information has come to light that makes it imperative she be kept away from the Peabody house at all costs."

"And how bad would it be if I said that she might be there right now?"

Slam.

The abrupt hanging up had Dale's blood turning cold. "Drive faster. Brenda's in deep shit."

Chapter Seventeen

So getting eaten by a house proved less painful than expected. It didn't involve any actual chewing of my body parts or gross digestive juices.

However, I did find myself in an odd dilemma.

More like an odd place.

"I don't think I'm in Kansas anymore," I said, channeling my favorite old movie. Nor did I have Toto, or any of my dogs with me.

I could have used them for moral support.

A glance around showed me somewhere surreal. A mostly gray landscape, rocky and barren, the ground a jagged stone that humped unevenly. Behind me, a taller pile of rock loomed, along with the slit I'd gotten spat out of. Should I pop back in?

Would shoving myself through that gap take me back into the house, or would something a little more dire happen? How did I know this wasn't the mouth of a beast?

That girl in *Temple of Doom* might have braved sticking her hand in that hole, but I still remembered the shivering horror of those bugs crawling over her. I couldn't do it.

Besides, shouldn't I explore just a little?

A warm breeze with hints of sulfur fluttered at my skin, a rotten smell that made my nose wrinkle. Would I asphyxiate if I breathed it too long? My lungs didn't hurt. Not yet.

Whoosh.

A sudden burst of flames from the ground drew a squeak from me, and it echoed in the stillness. Way to draw attention to myself. For once, that didn't seem like the brightest idea.

Whatever lived in this place might be all too interested in a human girl who'd wandered somewhere she shouldn't have.

A bigger dilemma than the one of whether or not human flesh was considered a tasty treat was, where should I go? What should I do?

The movies I'd seen involving people getting sucked into weird alternate universes without fail had people trying to get home.

With that thought in mind, I whirled to face the crack, ready to wedge myself in and hope the house regurgitated me. I'd brave the black hole to return to my rightful world.

That was the plan until I noticed a pair of red eyes peeking at me from the top of the stony crag.

Those crimson orbs, I might add, peered out from the face of a tiny gray gargoyle perched over the dark slit.

The size of a kitten, and a fugly kind of cute, I crooned. "Hey, cutiekins, aren't you just adorable. Want to come back with me?" I'd been talking about getting a pet, and I didn't know anyone who owned an alternate dimension gargoyle.

It made a cooing sound that drew me closer.

A second head popped up. Another gargoyle, much larger this time, but just as craggily adorable.

I reached out a hand, and the big one opened its mouth, revealing a row of teeth, but it was the way it unhinged its jaws and showed a second layer of sharp incisors that made me snatch my hand back, that and the lisped, "Supper!"

Oh, hell no.

I had two choices as it unfurled its wings. Dive for the slit and hope I didn't get wedged—because if I did, that little monster would probably feast on my ass—or run. Since I rather liked my butt, guess what I chose.

Whirling around, I bolted and immediately regretted my choice as the pebbles underfoot rolled, upsetting my balance. The cracks zigzagging through the arid soil sought to twist my ankles. The uneven surface tried to trip me. As if all that wasn't annoying enough, flying around in circles overheard, chirping, was my little gargoyle buddy and his papa.

Big papa wasn't even pretending I had a chance.

Had to be a male to taunt me so.

The overcast sky lent a shadowy pallor to the land, making it hard to discern much, but as I ran, I noticed what appeared to be a building in the distance. Shelter.

With a door.

I pounded on it, noting the gray and weathered age of the wood bound into a rectangle by bands of metal. There was a handle that didn't do shit when yanked.

The bigger gargoyle—that I nicknamed Butthead—fluttered overhead with a keening cry before perching on the crumbling stone edge of the roof. A two-story tower on the edge of nowhere. Little Butt wobbled as it landed beside its daddy. A predator in training.

When the door opened, and I saw the light shining within, I might have sobbed in relief.

Then backed away.

"Um, yeah, sorry to have bothered you. Wrong house. I think I'll be leaving now."

The hulking demon, with curling horns and bright red eyes, grinned. "Master will be happy to see you."

Lovely. How had I gone from no one wanting me to everyone?

Fuck.

Pivoting, I didn't figure there was much chance of me escaping. Butthead had obviously herded me here. But I tried anyway, running once again—despite my protesting legs—only to find myself plucked into the air, legs still pumping but not getting me anywhere.

And the big brute who'd captured me took me into his lair.

Chapter Eighteen

Okay, so it wasn't Butthead's lair. But at the time, I didn't know it. All I knew was he carried me into a weird place with things that made no sense.

Like the rose-colored carpet on the floor, lumpy and curling at the edges, stained by dust.

A dining room set, the wood also covered in a patina of gray—indicating a strong need for a maid or, at least, a vacuum.

More things I recognized dotted the room, such as a television, and stereo, both silent. It took only a moment for my brain to have a light-bulb moment.

These were the missing items from Peabody's house. He wasn't completely crazy.

I, on the other hand, might be a little off-kilter because, sitting on a throne at the far end of the room, was a man. Not a demon. Or a monster. Not even a guy with horns and a tail, but a hottie of epic proportions.

Flame-red hair, a smirk on his lips, and a red spark in his eyes. His alabaster skin smooth, his body lean and dressed in faded black leather.

"If it isn't Miss Brenda Jane Whittaker."

He knew my name. That couldn't be good. "Hi." It seemed rude to say nothing.

"I've been hearing a lot about you lately."

What had he heard? Good stuff? Bad? Did I care? "Oh, like what?" I played it safe.

"You're the direct descendent of Jasmine Baker. Or, as we used to call her before she escaped this hell, Jas'a'meen Ba'ak'ra, which translates to she who bakes the blood of her enemies."

I blinked because I knew the first name he mentioned. "Are you talking about Meemaw?" My sweet little meemaw?

"So you admit to being related to her?"

"She's my grandma."

"Twice removed heir." He sniffed the air. "I can smell her faintly on your skin."

"Which is kind of gross considering I showered." And I hadn't seen Meemaw since she'd left on her cruise a few weeks ago.

"We've been waiting a long time to find her again."

"Hate to break it to you, but you still technically haven't. I mean, I'm here, she's not, and given I'm pretty sure you're not on any map, it's doubtful she'll find me." No one would find me. Even my wolfie lovers, if still interested, would have a hard time sniffing my trail into Hell.

"We don't need her to come to us. You were kind enough to heed our call."

"What call? I'm pretty sure I didn't answer any numbers from Hell recently." If it had 666 in it, I knew better than to say hello.

"You were lured here as part of my plan. You are the key I need to escape this place."

"Key?" I looked down at myself. "I'm pretty sure I don't fit in any lock." More like people inserted things into me, not the other way around, but I wasn't about to mention that to the freaky, redheaded dude.

"On the contrary, you are the thing I've been searching for."

"Does this mean you're the one who has been possessing people?"

"Not me." His face crinkled with disgust. "Even if ruling in disgrace, I do have some standards. My minions, on the other hand, have been taking over and driving the human bodies we've appropriated until they break. Invariably, all you weak humans break, even with proper feeding. You can't contain our mighty essences for long. But your blood will change that."

"My blood isn't special. It's not even rare." Not that I did my civic duty and donated often. Meemaw felt very strongly about blood banks, and so I abstained.

"On the contrary, your blood is very special. Or did you not pay attention? You are a blend of *daemon* and human." He gave it an odd inflection.

"I am not a demon."

"Not a full-blooded one. Just a quarter-breed, and found by the luckiest of chances. And to think you almost fed one of my minions."

"Who?" And yet, I could guess. Who but Mrs. Peabody had eyed me with such strange hunger?

"It matters not how you came to me, the

fact of the matter is that you are mine to use now. Your essence, while diluted, should be exactly what I need to survive outside this plane of existence. If I imbibe enough of it, enough to change my own blood, I shall be able to cross to your world without needing the body of another."

Of all the things this handsome—yet apparently not human—man told me, one thing stood out, and it wasn't the fact that he wanted my blood to invade Earth.

Meemaw's a demon!

Holy shit. That probably explained her gruff personality and the fact that we'd never had a pet. But given that she even lived outside Hell meant she'd siphoned someone's blood first.

Someone like me.

"Put out your hand."

I tucked my arms behind my back. "Hold on a second. Let's not be hasty. I mean, how do you know it's even good enough?"

"I can smell it."

Again, totally gross. "Can't you get it from somewhere else?"

"If I could, I wouldn't need you. Hold her still," he ordered.

The big brute who'd answered the door grabbed me tightly, and I could only watch as a slimmer demon, his skin a grayish green, his eyes drooping in his sagging face, approached, a knife in one hand.

"Aren't you going to use a needle?" I asked.

"No."

"Have you at least sterilized that thing? I

don't want to catch a demonic infection," I babbled, my mouth being the only thing I could move.

"You won't die. I need you, and when I'm done transforming, then your blood will feed the army I shall raise."

"Army? For what?" I asked, wincing as the blade drew a deep line on my arm. Blood welled in the cut. Bright red, the brightest thing in this place other than my sparkling personality.

"To conquer your world, of course. I shall call a legion to my banner. Feeding them the taint of your human blood, crossed with that of a powerful demon, we shall cross the rift that has formed between our worlds."

Since watching myself bleed out really sucked, I tried to focus on more interesting things. "How did a hole to your world form inside the Peabodys' house anyhow?"

The red-haired dude, who had yet to give me his name, watched as my blood dripped into a chalice. "The rift occurred by chance. Our planes lie very close to each other, constantly rubbing, and if rubbed enough, a crack forms, but not for long. Once detected, there are those who would repair it instead of leaving it open that we might cross."

"But I thought you couldn't go over because our world doesn't agree with you?" I felt faint and slightly nauseous at the amount of blood spilling from me.

"That doesn't stop us from entering your world as incorporeal beings who must attach ourselves to a human host. So long as my kind feed, they can usually prevent a host from rejecting the spirit."

"That's why they've been going after the witch blood?"

"Blood imbued with magic sustains the host and makes the rider stronger."

In other words, we could starve those who seemed possessed and eject the demons from their bodies. I had to tell someone, but how? I was kind of caught for the moment.

"What happens if the host dies while the demon is in it?"

"Then the spirit snaps back into this realm."

"You mean those demons don't die?"

A slow smile pulled his lips. "We are not so easy to kill."

"If you can ride a human,"—which sounded so much better when it involved sex and not possession—"why are you still here?"

A sneer pulled his lip upward. "That mode of transport is for minions. Lords such as I are above such things. And why settle for the body of another when I can drink of your blood and enter your world at full strength?"

"Why do you want into my world so badly?"

He blinked. "Because."

"Because why? Why not just rule this world?"

"It's not possible." His lips flattened.

"How is it not possible? I mean, you're some kind of lord, right, with servants and shit? Why not form an army and declare yourself king?"

"There is already a supreme ruler."

My eyes widened as I understood his dilemma. "You're only a little demon on the scale, aren't you? No wonder you want to rule mine. Well, you're in for a surprise, buddy, because humans aren't that easy to squash."

"You have been so far."

"Because we didn't know you existed. Once you start mucking around too much, though, you'll see. Humans will converge, and probably the Lycans and vampires—"

"Vampires!" He spat the word. "The ultimate betrayers. We created them to serve us and bring us what we needed from your world. Instead, they deserted us."

"Is it me, or don't you get along with people?"

"Why should I?"

"Is this because your mother didn't hug you as a child?"

"My mother died in an uprising led by my father."

"So, what you're saying, is this is a family tradition."

"This is my destiny!" He thumped his chest and, for a moment, he looked very human—if you ignored the crazy eyes and the fact that he wanted to rule the world.

Then again, as a little girl, I, on my pink Power Wheels, with my army of Barbies, had wanted to do the same thing.

"Maybe you should rethink your destiny, given it hasn't been working out so well for you."

"Gag her!"

A slimy hand slapped over my mouth, and I could only hope he meant what he said about keeping me alive.

The dude collecting my blood had finally stopped and placed some kind of bandage over my wound.

"With this essence, I shall rule!" The redheaded underlord—because he certainly wasn't over anyone out here—held up the chalice and chugged it.

Gross.

He, on the other hand, loved it and smacked his lips. What could I say? I tasted that good.

"I feel myself changing already."

"Then we're done."

"We've barely even begun."

According to him, this was only the start. He wanted to keep draining me of blood, first to cement his ability to walk on Earth and then to feed his army. Not exactly my idea of a great future.

There was only one thing to do.

Faint, which was easier than faking an orgasm with an inept idiot.

I slumped to the floor beside my satchel and heard the underlord curse. "Did you take too much blood, you fucking moron?"

"Humans are always weak, master. She will need time to recover."

"I don't want to wait."

"If you continue to drain her, then she will

most likely die."

"Arrrrggh." Thump. *Bang*. Someone had a lovely tantrum.

Given the doctor's orders, I kind of hoped they'd all wander away and leave me alone, but a barked, "Throw her in a cell," meant I had to act.

When the big doofus went to grab me, I stopped faking. Out came the pepper spray, and what do you know, their giant red eyes were just as sensitive to it as a guy who couldn't keep his hands to himself.

The big demon bellowed, and the redheaded wannabe world ruler yelled for someone to grab me. The demon who'd taken my blood replied, "All of our other soldiers are recovering from their excursion to the Earth plane." I took advantage of the chaos and took off.

I ran for the door, bolted outside it, and headed for the slit, my legs pumping hard. Look at me becoming a kickass marathoner.

I just had to make it to the rift.

Of course, Butthead just had to harass me. The gargoyle dove at me, and I covered my face to protect it, blocking my visibility. I tripped and hit the ground hard on my arm.

Fuck.

I popped back up to my feet. Butthead came swooping in, and I swung my satchel.

Wham, it went wheeling into the ground, and I started running again.

Up ahead, I could see the rocky mound and the dark crack in it.

I can make it. I know I can.

"Halt." The magical command fisted me tightly, and I shrieked.

It was quite girly and unlike me, but it had an interesting effect. The invisible hand holding me vanished.

Whirling on one heel, I faced the underlord. He looked a touch pissed.

His eyes glowed brightly, but he didn't have smoke coming from his nose or ears.

I wasn't done yet. I yanked off my cross and held it in front of me like a talisman.

"Stay back, foul creature," I shouted.

His lip pulled up at one corner. "Do you really think that will stop me?"

Nope. But his eyes couldn't help but follow the shiny object, which meant he wasn't watching my knee.

Smoosh. Demon balls were as susceptible as human ones.

As he hunched over, gasping, I turned and dove for the slit in the rock.

The house spat me out, right at some feet. I recognized the shoes.

I looked up and grinned. "Hey, Scooby. Nice of you to bring the gang."

Was it too much to ask that they kiss me instead of shaking me to say hello?

Sebastian Interlude

Usually an easygoing guy, Sebastian was the first to react, hauling Brenda off the floor and shaking her. "What the fuck were you thinking?"

Before she could reply, a rarity, Dale took a turn. "Do you have any idea how worried we were!"

Then it was Mike, who only shook her once with a muttered, "Moron," before hugging her close with a softer, "Thank fuck you're safe."

Brenda hugged him back and proclaimed, "Mike is still my favorite."

Dale shook his head. "Seriously? What if I said I had donuts in the car?"

She threw herself at Dale and hugged him. "New favorite."

It made Sebastian wish he had a chocolate bar on him so he could be next. He got his hug without one. Brenda slipped her arms around him for a squeeze.

"Thanks for coming, but we probably should go. There's an angry demon coming after me."

"He can't follow." Morfeus entered the house in full wizard regalia, his long, dark robes brushing the rotting floor. "They can only possess humans who don't have any magic in their blood." The grand Whizziar was followed by several other wizards in robes.

"Brenda's human." Dale eyed her with a frown.

She planted her hands on her hips. "Are you trying to say something, Scooby?"

Morfeus waved a hand. "The female is not carrying a demonic parasite. She can't because her foul existence repels them."

"My foulness repels?" She turned her temper on Morfeus. "There is nothing repellent about me, Merlin."

"Morfeus."

"Whatever. I'll have you know that the reason a demon isn't humping my brain is because, according to them, my blood is very tasty. So yummy in fact, that my demon host on the other side drank a great big cup."

At the mention, Morfeus's eyes widened. "You fed a demon your tainted essence?"

"Not on purpose. But yes."

"Get out!" Morfeus screamed. "Everyone out, now. "

Since Brenda opened her mouth, probably to ask a thousand new questions, Sebastian hoisted her over a shoulder and they fled the house, a building that heaved and moved underfoot. Groaned as if stretching itself.

As they fled out the door, Sebastian heard a voice from behind say, in a tone more deserving of a mansion than a crumbling heap, "Won't anyone stay to welcome their new ruler?"

"Return to your dimension," Morfeus demanded, the warm air of his command blasting past Sebastian.

Magic. There was only one thing to do about magic.

Get as far away as you could.

Sebastian paused only to wrench the door open. He dove over the threshold and hit the yard, where some of the wizards had stretched in a line, hands raised, chanting.

A red glow emanated from their fingers, and Sebastian thought it best to get behind the line of fire.

Dale and Mike joined him on the sidewalk, where Sebastian deposited Brenda, who declared, "Your ass is fascinating to watch when you run."

"What's happening?" Willow came running, leaving the driver's side of her Smart car open.

"I think I caused an apocalypse." Brenda beamed.

"What she means to say is, apparently, a demon of some kind managed to cross over without needing a human body."

"A full demon? Without a circle to contain it?" Willow's eyes widened.

"I take it that's bad," Mike said.

Brenda made a *pshaw* sound. "The wizard dudes will handle it." Indeed their spell casting had reached a crescendo, and red light, sizzling and dancing like flames in the air, shot from their fingertips and hit the house.

It immediately caught fire and began to burn. But it didn't burn quietly. It moaned and screamed, the sounds eerie and blood-chilling.

"What's happening?" Brenda asked. "It sounds like the house is hurting."

"In a sense, it is. The souls of the human hosts caught between the worlds are escaping their prison."

"Going back to their bodies?"

Willow shook her head. "Unfortunately not. This will simply prevent new incursions."

"What about the ones still on Earth?"

"A hunt is underway to find them. The demons will be sent back to their dimension."

Fantastic news, except the man with the flaming red hair and even redder eyes strode from the house, unbothered by the flames, his lips stretched wide in a smile.

"Peasants of Earth, bow to your new leader."

"That's the dude who drank my blood." Brenda pointed just to make sure everyone knew who she meant.

"I, the great Lord An'al'onious"—Brenda wasn't alone snickering at his anal name—"have come to rule your world."

"Begone, foul creature!" Morfeus shot a jagged streak of lightning at the demon.

He held up a hand and absorbed it. "Did no one ever tell you that demon magic, being the root of all magic, is stronger than that of any other?" He swept a hand and bowled the wizards over. A flick of his hand and their arms were wrenched behind their backs. The wizards' mouths hung open, but not a sound emerged. "You'll make delicious meals for my minions. Stay here while I fetch my prize."

What prize? "What's he talking about?"

"Oh, shit, I think I know," Brenda mumbled. She lurched into a run, and it took only a half second to realize what the demon was after.

Sebastian threw himself in the path, as did Dale and Mike. They all tried to grab hold of the demon that gave all indications of being a man on fire.

He burnt like fire, too. The touch of him singed the skin on their hands. A flick of his hand, and they were thrown away.

In but a moment, the fiery male had Brenda, his hand wrapped around her hair, not burning her but not gentle either.

She fought, twisting and turning, cussing him out. "Let me go, you bastard."

"Not yet. I have need of you. Need of your blood. One cup was not enough, and I am losing my thread with this world." Indeed, the demon intruder's skin rippled. His entire being waved.

He drew Brenda up on tiptoe and, with his other hand, slashed a line. A thread of red appeared on her neck.

The demon bent its head and—

"Unhand the girl." A shriveled little woman dressed in a flowered muumuu appeared out of nowhere to give that order.

The red gaze flicked toward the new arrival and smirked. "Do you really think I'm frightened of a human witch?"

"Who said I was a witch? How easily the children of the other realm are fooled." The old lady smiled, and a spark appeared in her eyes, a spot of red that grew. "You shouldn't have touched my grandchild." With a flick of her fingers, the demon, with his mouth hanging open, exploded into a cloud of dust, setting Brenda free.

And she just couldn't be scared for once. Nope. She smiled wide and squealed, "Meemaw! You're home."

Chapter Nineteen

I hugged my grandma, so happy to see her, even if I now knew she was a demon. I didn't care. This woman loved me.

Which was why she harangued me.

"Two weeks, Brenda. Two weeks I was gone." Despite her short stature, when Meemaw wagged a finger, you paid attention. "Couldn't you stay out of trouble that long?"

Too many people shouted, "No!"

How well they all knew me.

Meemaw scowled. "A good thing our boat hit that reef and we flew home early, or who knows what mischief would have occurred."

"The world domination idea wasn't mine, Meemaw. Blame him." I pointed to the puddle of dust. "Cool spell. Can you teach me?"

"Teach you magic?" It wasn't just Meemaw that managed to look appalled.

I'd work on her later. "How come I never knew I was part demon? How come all demons don't look like demons? Or do you?" I tried to peek around at Meemaw's butt.

"What are you doing, child?"

"Checking for a tail."

"I don't have a tail. And neither do you,"

she added before I could peek at my backside.

"Are you a body snatcher?" I asked. Because if she was, we'd probably have to go on the run. Those snooty wizards wouldn't get my meemaw.

"This is my body. No one else's."

"But you're a demon, not a human."

"Correct. I migrated here from the other realm. And before you ask, the reason I don't look grotesque is because only the lower classes let themselves go. I was born a princess."

"So does that mean I'm special?" My shoulders went back.

"You were always special, granddaughter." Meemaw's gaze softened before hardening. "But you're still an idiot. How am I supposed to leave you alone for some me time when you're always getting into trouble?"

I rolled my eyes. "I was working a case."

"A case that involved you getting your blood siphoned by a demon lord and wizards."

"You. The collective wants a word with you, Jasmine Baker."

"I haven't the time to speak to you."

"I demand you—" Meemaw's upraised hand took care of the grand whizzer and his demands. He froze in place, mouth open wide, not a sound emerging.

Meemaw frowned. "Pompous idiots. And this is why I don't advertise our roots. I have no interest in dealing with their ilk, which means we'll have to move."

"Move?" I gaped. "But I don't want to

leave."

"And I can't very well leave you alone."

"Would it help, ma'am, if we volunteered to look out for her?"

Her dark gaze perused my boys—war-torn, handsome, and here to rescue me, boys.

"All three of you?"

They didn't even pause they nodded so fast. My va-jay-jay rejoiced by wetting my, until now, dry underpants.

"She'll need careful watching."

"The closest," Dale agreed.

"She's not a whore. You'll have to claim her."

"As soon as we get her somewhere safe, ma'am."

Meemaw's lips pursed. "Very well. I approve."

"Thank you!" I flung my arms around my grandmother's neck and hugged her tightly.

"Anything to keep you safe, child." She whispered, "Now, forget."

"Forget what..." I blinked and found myself standing on the sidewalk outside the Peabodys' house.

"What just happened?" I asked.

"Brenda!" I found myself grabbed and shaken, the moment having a déjà vu feel to it. "What the fuck were you thinking?" asked Sebastian.

Before I could think of replying, Dale took a turn trying to give me whiplash. "Do you have any idea how worried we were!"

For some reason, I could mouth along in perfect time when Mike shook me next and muttered, "Moron."

I broke the cycle after that, freaked out, and was still so confused.

Last I recalled, I'd entered the Peabody house then…nothing. I certainly didn't recall the house being on fire.

Did I do that?

"What's happening here?" The grand whizzer Morfeus piled out of a giant dark blue Suburban with his posse of wizards. The robes were too funny—and also seemed familiar.

I couldn't help but ask, "Dude, did you like get those on special from a Harry Potter Discount store?"

"Lycan, your female is impertinent and infringing on an active collective investigation."

"Investigation of what?" Dale pointed to the house. "Looks like the problem has been solved."

Had it? I felt like there was something more, something I should remember.

Yet when I tried to poke, my mind gave me a slap and I heard Meemaw's voice barking, "Leave it alone."

So I did.

Except for one thing. "I don't suppose anyone has donuts?" Because I really had a craving for one.

Looking up the street, I noticed Willow sitting in a Smart car. Stupid tiny things. Give me a beast truck with a metal frame any day.

Willow and her pathetic excuse for a car put-putted off, and as it drove past, her eyes never once veering to peek at us, I noticed in her back window a tiny orange cat.

Made sense. She was, after all, a witch.

"What is she doing here?" Morfeus whined.

"*She* probably solved this case." Even if I couldn't remember how.

"Did you do this?" He pointed at the flames.

I could, in all honesty, say, "Don't recall as I did."

"Well, someone did and—" Morfeus went off on a tangent.

Nobody listened. Nobody of import at any rate. His lackeys might have to listen, but we didn't.

Since the grand whizzer was busy being a douchebag, my boys, yes, my boys—a certainty that I couldn't explain where it came from—bundled me off without even asking. They took me home, and by home, I mean their place.

I allowed Mike to drive Big Blue, which despite their claims of being broken started just fine. I was kind of jealous when Mike declared her the most beautiful thing he'd ever seen. After me, of course.

Good save.

Not much was said on the drive over, surprising for me. I kept turning over and over in my head what had happened. Or more like, what didn't happen?

Why did it feel as if I'd lost a chunk of

time?

Forget…

The hot spray of the shower helped ease some of my tension, and the longer I kept my face in the water, the more my stress eased.

What was I freaking out about? Nothing happened.

Forget.

Nothing at all.

The Peabodys' house had burnt to a crisp, and here I was, naked in a shower, and if I wasn't mistaken, a man wearing just a towel stood outside the stall waiting for me.

I stepped out into a warm and fluffy embrace, the towel, not the man. The hug from my man was hard and hot and smelled so good.

"How did you get clean?" I said, sniffing his neck.

"You didn't really think this was the only bathroom, did you?" The corners of Dale's eyes crinkled.

"Where are the other boys?"

"Still sluicing off."

"Right here," Mike announced, stepping into the bathroom, his wet hair slicked back, his torso still damp, the towel hanging dangerously low on his hips.

This day was getting better and better.

"Don't you have to work?" I asked.

"We took the day off."

"We had more important things to do."

"Oh." Me, playing coy. I loved it. "Like what?"

"You, of course," announced Sebastian, peeking his head through the door. "And can we move this to the bedroom? It's got a bed."

"What makes you think I want to return to it?" I tilted my chin.

"Don't even try to pretend you don't," growled Dale. "You know what's going to happen."

"Dirty, bad things, I hope." I winked. "Last one there has to come in my mouth."

Which, in retrospect, probably wasn't an incentive to get there fast. I splayed myself on the bed and waited.

And waited.

I finally had to yell, "I'm going to masturbate if you guys don't get in here," before they pushed and shoved their way through the door.

Then they paused.

"So, we kind of want to apologize,"

"For leaving the toilet seat up?" I asked.

"No."

"For not having more donuts for the ride home?"

"No."

"For letting me wake up all alone and thinking you didn't like me?" I threw that at them and watched them flinch.

"We didn't mean for that to happen. Someone left a shitty note." Dale glared at Mike.

He shrugged. "If you wanted pretty, you should have asked Sebastian."

"If it's any consolation, had we not been

called away, this morning would have gone much differently," Sebastian offered.

"A lot different," Dale added. "We never meant for you to think we weren't coming back."

"Or that we used you."

"What these fucktards can't seem to say is we care for you and want to claim you, all three of us, if you'll have us. Or you can choose just me. I am, after all, the nicest one of the bunch."

At that, we all stared at Mike.

He scowled deeper than usual. "I am. Just because I don't smile often doesn't mean shit."

For once, I showed caution. "And if I do say yes to all three, what does that mean?"

"You'll be ours forever."

Be still my beating heart. Wait a second. I didn't want to be undead. So I clapped instead. "Okay."

"That's it? Okay? Don't you have more questions?"

If he insisted. "Does it hurt?"

"A bit. We have to leave a mark."

"Really?" My grin widened. "Can you make it really visible so I can show it off at work?"

"This isn't a joke."

"I wasn't kidding. This is how I am, take it or leave it. That means the questions and the teasing. And me saying inappropriate things like, who's picking up the wolf poo in the yard, and no coming inside smelling of wet dog, and would it be okay if I got you matching collars and leashes and took you on the occasional walk."

That earned me an emphatic "No!"

"Spoilsports."

"Don't you have any serious questions? Once we do this, there's no turning back."

"Will you ever leave me?" Probably the one question that really mattered.

And they were of one voice and one mind when they said, "Never."

"Good, because I'm ready to settle down." More than ready. "Now, as to my warning, I will move in here since it's got more room than my place. You'll each give me a chunk of closet. I might not be into a foursome every night, but if I do singles, then be sure I'll treat you fairly. Oh, and I like to cook. And eat. A lot. Any comments about my weight or eating habits will see you not getting eaten." I mimed a blowjob in case they didn't get the hint. "Any questions?"

They blinked at me. Probably in awe of my management skills. Wait until we had sex again. They'd only barely skimmed the surface of the things I wanted to try.

Tonight would be a foursome night. Maybe that would be our Wednesday night thing. And Friday, definitely Saturday so I could walk bowlegged into brunch and totally have something to brag about.

"Now, if we're done talking, can we get to more interesting things like fucking?" I beckoned.

Dale came, not literally, not yet, but he did approach the bed, as did the other two men, taking up positions around me.

My harem.

Mine.

Leaning back, I pulled loose the towel and gave them a come-hither smile that worked like a charm.

I sighed as Sebastian flicked one of my fat nipples. The tease.

"Suck it," I ordered.

"Yes, ma'am." He dove onto me, latching on tightly, making me arch with a cry.

"The other nipple is getting jealous," I remarked, which led to a second mouth attaching itself.

Yes. And a thank you to Dale.

Mike was a god among wolves. He massaged my calves, kneading my muscles, working his way up my leg as the other two sucked and flicked my taut pebbles.

Pure heaven. My fingers threaded into their hair, holding them close to me. Already, my body hummed, pleased at their sensual caresses, hungry for more.

Mike reached the top of my thigh, and I clenched, expecting his touch, only to moan as he started on the other leg, caressing his way up again while the other two sucked and nibbled at my flesh.

Sexual excitement coiled within me, each stroke of their hands, each caress from their mouths, raising my pleasure higher and higher.

My pussy ached, wet and eager, clenching and unclenching, wondering why there wasn't a cock in there filling it up.

"I think she's ready," Mike said, having reached the top of my thigh. His fingers brushed against my damp sex, and I cried out.

"Who's going first?" Sebastian asked.

"Me." Dale, take-charge Scooby, flopped onto his back beside me, and next thing I knew, Mike and Sebastian had me poised over his cock.

With their hands on my waist, I straddled Dale, the tip of his dick tickling my clit. It felt so good. I couldn't help but grab him and rub him more firmly.

"Fuck me," Dale hissed, his hips arching.

"If you insist," I replied before slamming myself down on his dick.

Oh, my. There was something about a rapid fill, a quick stretch that excited me. My head tilted, my wet hair dangling down my back, my fingers digging into the sheets for balance as I rocked on his cock.

I leaned forward and palmed his chest, grinding myself against him, driving him deep, so deep.

And my excitement didn't just come from the pleasure of him filling me, but from knowing I had an audience, a participating one. Their hands were on my body as I moved, helping me to rock, tugging at my nipples, playing with my ass, one even daring to slide between our bodies to stroke against my clit.

A hand in the middle of my back pushed me forward, and a body pressed against me, a hard cock trapped in the crevice between my cheeks. It slid back and forth, a sensual slide of bodies and skin.

My lips found Dale's for a kiss as I gyrated

faster, my orgasm hovering so close.

But his was closer. I felt him spurt inside me, hot and wet, and I started to come, too, ripples of it that were stopped dead when he whispered, "Be mine, kitten," and bit me.

Ouch. It pinched and then spread pleasure through me unlike anything. My orgasm rolled through me and wasn't done when I found myself flipped onto my back, my legs held up so they hung over Sebastian's shoulders.

My body spread wide, the tip of his dick teased me before plunging into my still quivering flesh.

"Oh." What else could I say? I barely had any breath to speak as he thrust into me oh so hard, driving me like a piston, faster and faster.

But I'd just come. I needed a little more help. As Sebastian thrust in and out of me, he slid his hands between our bodies, found my clit, and pinched it.

Holy fuck. I screamed and arched as my orgasm came crashing back, my sex squeezing his cock so tightly it wrung a climax out of him. Sebastian shuddered as he came and flopped heavily onto me, his lips finding my neck, and this time, I was prepared for the sharp bite and the euphoria that followed.

Floating on cloud nine, I nonetheless knew I wasn't quite done. I shoved Sebastian off to the side and opened my heavy eyes to see Mike standing between my legs, stroking his thick and hard cock.

Oh, my.

I beckoned him nearer as I scrambled to my knees. We faced each other on the bed, close enough I could reach out to drag a fingernail down his chest. I didn't stop at his waist but kept on tracing right down to his groin then around it, doing my deliberate best to avoid his straining cock.

Tease me with his massage, would he? Two could play that game. Besides, it was really hot the way he couldn't control his ragged breathing.

As I reached out to grab his balls, holding their heavy weight in my palm, a body pressed against my back.

For a second, as I cupped Mike, I leaned into Dale's, my body tingling as his hands reached around to grab my breasts, his thumbs brushing my nipples.

But Dale had already gotten his turn. It was Mike's turn.

Dropping his sac, I reached for his cock and clamped it tight. I began to stroke him, fisting him tight, jerking him off fast and furious, enough that Mike's head tilted and he moaned.

Since this was time number three, I needed something unique, just for him. I'd done cowgirl and missionary. That left one more primary position.

Shoving myself away from both men, I put myself on my hands and knees. I waggled my ass.

Apparently, that was a clear invitation.

The fat head of a dick pushed against my slit and slid its way in until I sighed. Then squeaked as his thumb found my rosette and poked it.

"Mike!" I gasped his name.

He chuckled, the naughty man, and he finally laughed while he was sunk balls-deep into me with a thumb in my ass.

And I loved it.

I giggled in reply then quickly moaned as he began to fuck me, his shaft driving in and out of me, trying to stoke the fire that simmered.

But I'd come twice. I didn't know if I had it in me for a third.

Until a mouth latched onto my clit.

Dear, God.

I didn't know which of the two guys went to town on my nub, but with Mike thrusting into me, along with the lapping and flicking, next thing I knew, I was screaming—and coming. Then Mike was yelling and coming and biting.

And a good time was had by all.

So, being a smartass—a claimed smartass I might add—I just had to ask, "So, who's getting me some food?"

Smart men, they dove to grab some pants and run from the room.

This time, I didn't worry about them coming back.

They came, again and again, enough that I might walk bowlegged for a week.

Awesome!

I got so much exercise, I fell into a hard sleep that was rudely interrupted by a girlish scream.

I rolled over in time to see the clock showing an ungodly time of 5:40 a.m. and Dale diving to grab something to wrap around his hips. The reason for his sudden modesty?

Meemaw entered the bedroom.

"Meemaw, you're back from your trip early." Which oddly enough sounded familiar.

"How did she get in here?" Dale yodeled.

"I locked the door," Sebastian claimed.

Mike just stared at my meemaw. Who could blame him? She was pretty damned awesome.

"Hi, Meemaw." I waved.

"Don't you hi me, missy. What are you doing with these boys? I was worried to death until Chloe told me where to find you."

What was I doing? Monkey sex? Shattering windows with my screams? Trying to break some sexual records? Not things to tell my meemaw.

"I got married." Since I didn't have a ring, I proudly canted my neck to show her the marks.

She harrumphed. "About time you settled down. Although, did it have to be with canines?"

"How did you know they were wolves?" Was my meemaw more than just a sweet old lady with a viperish tongue?

"Chloe, of course, told me." Of course, my BFF did. Imagining my meemaw as more than a crotchety old lady was silly.

"I swear they're house trained."

Meemaw didn't bother to reply, but she did fix each of my boys in turn with an evil stare. "Hurt my Brenda, and I will ensure your soul suffers for an eternity."

While an odd threat, I couldn't help but wipe a tear at the sweetness of the sentiment.

Epilogue

The gaping hole at 999 Cloven Hoof Lane served as a reminder that Amityville-type houses could appear anywhere, even suburbia.

Despite the sifting of the house's remains, authorities never did find Mrs. Peabody's body, but the kids were recovered a few days later, several states over, without any memories of what they'd done. Had the demon hosts fled to another body or been chased back to their Hell world? No one could say for sure, but the hunt continued just in case.

Mr. Peabody never snapped out of his fugue state, which was probably for the best, considering the charges that would be leveled against him.

As for my wolf pack and me, even if I couldn't recall setting the house on fire, I knew I'd saved the city from evil.

Not bad for a secretary.

But did that mean my boys gave me any slack? Nope, they joined forces with my meemaw and spouted things like "menace to society," and that I was a danger to myself and others. My favorite rant of theirs, though, was when they told me I couldn't get hurt because I, Brenda Jane

Whittaker, was their reason for living.

They loved me. I loved them, and we were all living together in Dale's house, but not for long. We'd need a bigger place with an in-law suite. I wanted my meemaw close by, especially considering my secret.

Being me, I just couldn't reveal my surprise nicely, though. I stalked into the kitchen, the smells making me drool, and exclaimed, "Is it ready yet? Me and the babies"—yes, I said babies, as in twins!—"are getting hungry."

For big, tough guys, it didn't take much to lay them flat. I didn't mind, though. They loved me, foul mouth and all; even Meemaw tolerated them, and we were going to be one big happy fucking family.

Which, for some reason, made me think of cake.

Mmm. Cake. I wondered if someone would fetch me some. Oh, and some licorice, too. And...

*

Across town, Willow peeked out her window, looking for her cat, barely more than a kitten.

She'd not had him for long and only found him by chance, an orange stray who suddenly appeared in her life right around the time of the Peabody incident.

Where are you, furball? He never spent the night outside, preferring to snuggle under the blankets against her lower back.

When Whiskers didn't come, even after she shook the food bowl and made kissy noises, she ventured outside, wand in hand, incantation ready to fly.

What she saw sent her running back indoors to grab a phone and dial.

"Psychic Network, you need it, we know it," said the bored male who answered.

"This is a call for the TDCM," she stated.

Immediately, his tone changed. "How can I help you, ma'am?"

"I'd like to report a theft."

"Ma'am, this line is for serious magical emergencies. Theft and other petty crimes should be called in to the regular police."

"Not a normal kind of theft. I am fairly certain a demon stole my kitty."

"Why would you think that?"

Because of the clawed paw prints singed into her lawn.

The End but find out what happens next in:
A Demon Stole My Kitty.

For updates or to get to know me, visit my website, EveLanglais.com

CPSIA information can be obtained
at www.ICGtesting.com
Printed in the USA
BVHW01s0733271117
501320BV00002B/211/P